HIDDEN *talent*

Ria Alice and Jessica May

ISBN: 9781036929893

Playlist

"You're Losing Me (From The Vault)" - Taylor Swift
"1 step forward, 3 steps back" - Olivia Rodrigo
"Sex" - The 1975
"Heartbreak Girl" - 5 Seconds of Summer
"Why Don't You Love Me" - 5 Seconds of Summer
"goodnight n go" - Ariana Grande
"Magnet" - Picture This
"Being Your Friend" - Katherine Li
"he never will" - Alexander Stewart
"dandelion" - Ariana Grande
"Begin Again (Taylor's Version)" - Taylor Swift
"Fools" - Lauren Aquilina
"Please Don't Say You Love Me" - Gabrielle Aplin
"Ghost of You" - 5 Seconds of Summer
"Kill My Time" - 5 Seconds of Summer
"Crystal Clear" - Hayley Williams
"imperfect for you" - Ariana Grande

CONTENT NOTES

This story contains explicit sexual content, profanity and topics that some readers may find sensitive including mild violence.

1

AMELIA

"I haven't got time to argue about this now, I've just arrived. Alone. Thanks a lot Josh." I hung up the phone to my boyfriend, a mix of anger and disappointment swirled through my body as I reached the green door of Lilah and Zane's house.

You'd have thought after six years together, I would be used to Josh letting me down at the last minute but it still cut just as deep every time he made up yet another excuse to bail on me.

Josh and I met on a dating app and although I was usually drawn to a tall, dark and handsome man and Josh was the opposite, given his ash-blonde hair and shorter stature, his confident chat and charisma won me over. The first twelve months were a fairytale love story but as time ticked on it seemed the perfection began to crumble. Thus started the cycle of arguments, infidelity and broken promises.

Even I could admit our relationship hadn't been plain sailing but somewhere amongst the pain, there was a masochistic part of me that enjoyed the chaos.

What I didn't enjoy was standing in a room full of partygoers, many of whom I didn't know, dressed like an idiot, in one half of a couple's costume.

"It's really not that obvious you're part of a pair, babe." My friend, Jacob, reassured me with a shrug.

"I'm Thing fucking 2." I argued, taking a large swig of the alcohol in my plastic cup. "Who the fuck goes to a Halloween party dressed as *that* on their own?!"

"Well, if it's any consolation you look hot!" Said the perfect, doll-like Tinkerbell standing next to him. "Don't worry, I'm not in a couple costume either." Verity continued. We became friends a few years ago when Lilah started working with me and Jacob at Moreno Hart Jewellery. She starred in the blockbuster movie, *Accidentally in Love*, last year as the lead actor alongside her now-boyfriend, Axel Ford - who also happened to be one of the most famous men in the world! Since then, her star status had risen to unexpected heights but her humility remained the same.

"But at least he's here." I laughed. As the words left my mouth the crowd parted like the Red Sea to reveal the Hollywood heartthrob, dressed like an extra from *Top Gun,* in a khaki jumpsuit and aviator glasses.

"Hey, Tink," he winked at Verity, slinging an arm around her shoulder. Her cheeks glowed red as Axel pressed a kiss to the top of her head. "Will the other Thing be back flipping in soon?" He asked sarcastically, turning to me. Verity slapped him abruptly on the arm in a silent warning to shut up.

"Nope, just me tonight." I retorted, the declaration felt like a fresh stab wound as I had to repeat Josh's absence. Axel's eyes softened as if he immediately understood the situation. No doubt Verity had informed him of Josh's previous shortcomings over the course of their relationship.

"Hey, Axel, or should I say Maverick?" Jake joked, removing the spotlight from my solitude. "If there was an Oscar for Best Dressed at this party, you would win it in a landslide."

"Thanks a bunch, J." Noah, Jake's boyfriend, jested from his side. The pair of them were polar opposites. Where Jake was blonde and disorganised, Noah was brunette and meticulous. This was the first serious relationship I had witnessed Jake in. Although we had been friends for almost five years, he had always been more partial to playing the field rather than settling down, so for him to give that up, Noah must have been pretty special. Plus, I was certain he felt like he had won the lottery when he snagged the six-foot, rugby player-built accountant last year. "I thought you said I looked good in my zombie get up?"

"You do, babe," Jake confirmed, "but that's Axel Ford." He stage whispered, hiding his face from the movie star. To Axel's credit, he didn't seem uncomfortable by the flattery, rather he was amused by his girlfriend's taken aback expression.

"There they are!" Verity announced, waving in the direction of our hosts. Lilah and Zane glided through the throngs of revellers, looking the picture-perfect couple, until they reached our group.

"Hey guys, you all look amazing!" Lilah gushed. Her eyes narrowed in my direction, as if working out what or who I had come as.

"Don't ask," I waved her off.

"Thanks for coming, everyone." She continued, taking the hint. "We appreciate you making the effort."

"I've gotta ask buddy, what has Lilah promised you to wear that outfit?" Axel chuckled, referencing Zane's Roger Rabbit costume. It was an odd juxtaposition to see Zane so casual - not to mention the bunny ears! He had been my boss for several years, so I was more used to seeing him in perfectly pressed suits than oversized gaudy clothing.

"Delilah wanted to be Jessica Rabbit-"

"Verity wanted to be Tinkerbell but there was no chance I was putting on tights to be fucking Peter Pan." Axel cut him off, slapping him on the back with a chuckle.

"I think you look cute," Lilah kissed his cheek, looking a vision in red. Although he didn't show it, I'm certain Zane cringed at the compliment.

As I stood there as the seventh wheel amongst my melting pot of friends, surveying their happiness, I had never felt more isolated. It wasn't their fault, it wasn't on purpose and I was honestly overjoyed for each one of them, but their contentment only amplified the emptiness that was consuming me that evening.

"Are you fucking kidding me?!"

2

THEO

I stood frozen in shock, staring at the traitor across the room. For the majority of my life, we'd worn matching Halloween costumes but there he was in red fucking dungarees, whipped by my sister.

I marched towards him, barely able to contain my fury. "What the fuck is this?" I said, flicking his bunny tail. To my disgust, Zane had the audacity to laugh in my face along with his cackling sidekick, my little sister, Lilah. "We have a system! You wear your black suit, and I provide the accessories." I held up the trilby hat and black sunglasses as evidence, "and I kept *my* end of the deal."

"Sorry, T, I meant to tell you. She convinced me at the last minute." He snickered, pointing to Lilah. I'd hate to think about how she had convinced him, it was almost vomit inducing. Zane had been my best friend since we were kids, but since shacking up with my sister a few years ago, after working together brought them unexpectedly closer, I'd had to get used to the idea of the pair of them pretty quickly. Usually, their relationship didn't bother me in the slightest but fucking me over on Halloween took the biscuit.

"I have never felt more embarrassed in my life." I looked at the group of surprised faces, spotting Amelia clearly depicting one half of the famous Dr Seuss duo. "Now Amelia *and I* look stupid without our counterparts."

"Alright bloody hell, I think you'll be fine being a lone man in black," Amelia waved her hand dismissively.

"I'm a Blues Brother. I'm Jake and he's meant to be Elwood. There are two! So it doesn't work solo." I held my fingers up to emphasize the point.

I heard Axel snigger at my outburst before defending my point, "he ain't wrong. It does look stupid solo!" I held my hand out to emphasize my agreement, ignoring the obvious, playful dig.

"Oh, you'll get over it, Theo." Lilah rolled her eyes.

"Hm," I huffed before turning to Amelia. I plonked the trilby on her head. "Now we can be a couple, hey, Mils." She laughed slightly at my comment. I unfolded the arms of the sunglasses and slid them onto her heart-shaped face. Even in a baggy red top, tights and my clashing added-on accessories, she somehow still managed to be the most captivating person at the party.

I met Amelia when Lilah started working for Zane's company. Although she was working in Marketing at Moreno Hart Jewellery, she wrote a music blog on the side, called Under The Radar and was interested in discovering lesser-known musicians. After attending one of my band's, The Velvet Echoes, gigs she wrote an entry on her website which eventually led to us being booked to record the title track for Axel and Verity's movie. Since then, not only had our fame skyrocketed due to the success at the box office, but after Amelia's promotion we had begun to form a friendship based on our love and interest in music.

Although we didn't hang out regularly and she was firmly off the market, every time I was in her presence I was entranced by her beauty and quick wit. She was the coolest person I knew with her band tees and ripped denim, shoulder length butterfly braids and eclectic mix of two-toned jewellery.

"Great, now I look even worse." Amelia shook her head, looking somewhat like she'd been thrown up on by a fancy dress shop.

"Nah cutie, you pull it off." I winked jovially. "Let's go get you a drink." Something told me she needed one.

"Using those pet names is gonna get you in trouble one day." She sighed, slapping me on the arm. She'd told me on more than one occasion to keep my nicknames platonic, but it was in my nature to flirt with her. And although she claimed to hate it, it pulled a smile out of her every time.

We reached the in-house bar and I poured us two drinks before we found a corner of the room to occupy. Amelia kept taking her phone out of her matching red bag, checking the screen, grimacing and placing it back in the holder.

"Bored of me already? Counting down to your taxi home?" I handed her one of the cups.

"Huh?" Amelia glanced up from the phone screen, I flicked my gaze to her device before re-making eye contact. "Oh, no. I was seeing if Josh had messaged me." She shrugged, before taking the drink I was offering. It was clear he hadn't.

"I assume he was meant to be Thing 1?" I gestured to the badge on her chest emblazoned with her character name. "What possible reason could he have to stand you up and leave you thingless!"

She rolled her eyes at my attempt at a joke. "It's awful to admit but I'm not surprised. That's just Josh." She sighed. My heart sank slightly at her defeated voice as she confessed to accepting the bare minimum. I wanted to respond but I bit my tongue in fear that I wouldn't be able to stop the unsolicited advice from escaping.

I didn't know Josh well; in fact I'd only met him once at a dinner party in this very house last April but my opinion of him was less than positive. He struck me as the kind of man who wanted everything on his terms with no regard for consequences or anyone around him, particularly Amelia. From what I knew, they'd been together for years so I couldn't see the cycle breaking but it saddened me that she was putting up with way less than she deserved.

"Let's make a deal." She spoke animatedly, breaking me out of my thoughts, "if we're both ditched next year too, I'll be your Elwood." Her big brown eyes twinkled at me.

It was unlike me to wish for a girl to be stood up but in that moment, I couldn't help it. "I look forward to it," I clinked my glass to hers in agreement.

3

AMELIA

I peeled my eyes open to look around the dark room. There were bodies everywhere, still fast asleep surrounded by copious amounts of empty bottles. The stench of stale vodka hung in the air, intensifying the pounding in my head. I was thirty years old, I was definitely getting too old for crashing on a sofa after a house party!

Picking up my phone from the arm of the chair, I checked the time. It had just gone eight o'clock. Time to go I think! Absent-mindedly, I opened my text conversation with Josh. As expected, there had been no reply but he had seen my message at midnight. I tried not to dwell on the anxious feeling gnawing away at me. It wasn't unlike Josh to leave me on read and he always made it home in one piece, so I convinced myself that there was no use worrying further at this point.

Quietly, I slid off the sofa, gathered my belongings and made for the exit. The bright autumn sun blinded me momentarily as I opened the heavy door. I sat down on the front step, popped in my headphones and began plugging my pickup location into the Uber app. The crisp air and familiar tunes did wonders to bring me back to life.

"Walk of shame?" The male voice caused me to jump as he pulled on the wire of my headphones.

"Fucking hell, Theo!" I clutched my heart, "are you trying to kill me?"

"Sorry, Sunflower." He smirked, leaning against the door frame. The golden rays shone on his boyish face and caught on his hair, causing flecks of red to appear amongst the dark brown curls. I was suddenly hyper-aware of how crusty the makeup I had accidentally slept in must have looked and resisted the urge to rub my eyes.

"Why did you call me that?" I raised my eyebrow. Theo often threw around nicknames, but I hadn't heard him call me anything other than the generic ones.

"It reflects your sunny disposition." He winked before ruffling my hair and sauntering towards the multi-car garage. I pouted at the sarcastic compliment, my brain too soaked in alcohol to retort. I neglected to replace the earbud and leant back on my hands, closing my eyes, letting the cool breeze clear through my senses as I waited for the Uber to arrive. The crunch of gravel caught my attention.

Opening my eyes I was met with a shiny red sports car that I didn't recognise, stationary at the bottom of the stairs. Theo was flashing a cheesy grin, in my direction, from the driver's seat, before rolling down the window.

"Borrowing that from Zane?" I teased. The last time I saw Theo behind the wheel he was driving a ten-year old VW Polo, so this was quite the upgrade.

"Haven't you heard? I'm famous now!" Theo joked. If the words had come from anyone else, they would have sounded like a conceited arsehole, but from Theo, with that glint in his hazel eyes, all that was present was humour.

"Oh yeah! You're in Sean's band, right?" I tapped my chin pretending to think as I mentioned the lead singer of The Velvet Echoes.

Theo laughed, rolling his eyes. "Do you want a lift or not?"

I hadn't expected the offer, but I played it cool. "Is that your idea of an invitation?"

"My sincere apologies. Amelia Sani, would you do me the honour of allowing me to escort you home on this fine November morning?"

I stood up, slinging my bag over my shoulder and made my way down the stairs. "Okay, no need to beg," I giggled, opening the door and sliding into the passenger side. After clicking on my seatbelt, I cancelled the Uber and fully removed my headphones, tucking them into my pocket.

"Thanks, by the way." I smiled, grateful to not be still sitting on the cold concrete.

"Don't sweat it, sweet." He turned the music up slightly and I recognised the tune.

"Is this The Crystal Scars? I went to their gig the other week!" I gushed, turning to see Theo grinning at me.

"I may or may not be an avid follower of UTR." I felt my heart warm slightly at the mention of my blog. I knew he followed but I hadn't been aware that he paid any attention to the countless posts I uploaded about different indie bands.

"You a fan of them?" I asked, nibbling my bottom lip, I took the opinions of other people very seriously when it came to musicians I'd recommended.

"What does it sound like, Mils?" His laugh mixed with the unique melody of the song. We sunk into comfortable silence, just enjoying the music as the trees whizzed past us.

Although Theo and I were an unlikely duo and he drove me round the bend half the time, we had formed a strong friendship. Up until his band's discovery through my blog, I had dismissed him as just another fuckboy due to his multiple flirty advances in the past; however, after he reached out to thank me after booking the *Accidentally in Love* soundtrack, it appeared I had judged him unfairly. Behind the cheeky chappy was a man with a strong knowledge of music and a heart of gold. We didn't meet up regularly but whenever we did cross paths, I found myself inexplicably drawn towards him. He always had me dissolving into fits of giggles and I'd end up leaving with a smile on my face.

Surrounded by the noise of Lilah and Jake snoring in blissful sleep, I gave up trying to nod off and padded quietly through the kitchen of the dark flat.

I opened the fridge and perused for a midnight snack, settling on a strawberry yoghurt. Grabbing a spoon, I jumped up on to the counter and began to tuck in silently. My feast lit only by the orange glow from the streetlamps through the window.

My ears pricked up at the soft click of the door and before my fight or flight could kick in, I was flash banged as the room illuminated.

"Jesus Christ." A male voice cursed. I hopped off the side, brandishing the nearest weapon I could find. "Amelia?"

"God, I could have killed you!" I panted, clutching my chest as the image of Lilah's older brother became clear.

Theo laughed as he walked over to me, "what with a spoon covered in yoghurt?" He took the utensil out of my hand, disarming me with ease before placing it in his mouth and eating the excess.

I watched for a second as my pulse slowly returned to normal. "What are you doing here anyway?"

*"It's my apartment, cutie. What are **you** doing here?" He asked, passing back the spoon, which I promptly chucked in the sink. **I don't know where he's been.***

"Sleepover with Lilah and Jake but I was having trouble with the sleeping part." I shrugged.

"Figures," he chuckled, "do you need me to read you a bedtime story?"

*"No, I want to sleep, not be bored to death!" I joked, "black shirt and trousers," I assessed him, "back from a shift or auditioning for **Men in Black**?"*

"Shift, unfortunately." He loosened the knot of his tie, *"what about you? Lost your trousers at a Zeppelin gig?"* His eyes *grazed down my body, lingering on my exposed thighs, heat burned in their wake.*

Suddenly I was all too aware of the oversized band tee that I had worn to bed and nothing else. I nudged him playfully, "fuck off."

Theo opened the fridge, "beer? Seeing as you've already helped yourself to my food?" He held out a Moretti. I nodded sheepishly and he put the cap in between his teeth and opened the bottle.

"Is that how you open your customers beers at The Gilded Cage?" I teased, accepting the golden liquor.

"Only the ones I'm tryna impress."

"So, are you excited for your tour to start?" I asked, breaking the peace and shaking the memory of one of our earliest interactions out of my head.

"Huh?" Theo responded, his mind clearly elsewhere also, his almond-shaped eyes flicked between me and the road.

"The tour?" I asked again, The Velvet Echoes were set to start their first European tour in January and I hadn't had the chance to catch up with any of the members on how they were feeling about the milestone.

"Oh yeah! Can't wait!" He beamed, "Hope you've got your tickets ready!"

"I'm offended I'm not on the guest list, Theo." I laughed.

"Ah of course you are, Sunflower. I might even invite you backstage if you're lucky." He winked, I felt my cheeks warm at the obvious flirt and played with one of my braids.

"Careful, Theo." I warned, though my voice lacked venom. I knew that was just the way Theo spoke but sometimes his charisma caught me off guard. I wasn't used to that kind of male attention, and I refused to dwell on the unusual flutter in my gut when he made a joke that toed a little too close to the line. He chuckled beside me, his attention turning fully to the windscreen once again.

I began scrolling through my social media aimlessly, looking through countless pictures of Halloween costumes and revelry before my attention caught on a post from Tim, Josh's co-worker. The image was focussed on Tim, dressed as Batman, chugging a beer but my eyes were drawn to the figures in the back.

I felt my stomach drop.

There was my boyfriend with his arm slung around an unknown blonde, mouth inches from her face.

My breathing shallowed, my ears rang, and my hands felt clammy as I zoomed in on the grainy image, hoping my mind was playing tricks on me. So this was what was so much more important to him than spending the night with his long-term girlfriend!

"You okay, Mils?" The muffled sound of Theo's concerned voice briefly entered my consciousness before being wiped out by various scenarios rushing through my head.

I fought against the devil on my shoulder. I was needlessly jumping to conclusions. All I knew right now was that he had spoken to a girl, this picture didn't prove anything. I needed to speak to the man himself.

"Amelia?" Theo repeated as he shook my shoulder, breaking me out of my daze. I felt the car come to a complete stop.

"Yeah, yeah I'm fine. Thanks for the ride." I responded, realising the journey had ended. Feeling thankful in a way that I was now alone and free to call Josh to clear this up without an audience.

I scurried into my apartment, without glancing back at the road and clicked on Josh's contact the minute the door shut behind me. With each ring, my heart pounded harder as the internal battle between my rational and irrational thoughts fought on.

Eventually, I reached the answerphone. Not wanting to appear totally insane, I decided to give up for the minute and busy myself with removing my makeup and putting on some clothes that were less red!

An hour later, sans Halloween costume, I proceeded to try Josh again. This time to my surprise and delight he answered.

"Hello?" Josh croaked down the line, sounding as if I'd just woken him up. Relief washed over me as the sound of his voice confirmed he wasn't dead in a ditch somewhere.

"Hey, I'm glad to hear your voice." I sighed, flopping onto my sofa.

"Amelia? Jesus, what time is it?" His tone changed, sounding more alert, panicked almost.

"I was worried when I didn't hear back from you last night." It was only a half lie, the image of him and the blonde still very present in my mind.

"Don't be ridiculous, I'm fine." He responded, "I meant to message, but I passed out before midnight."

"You know me, I think the worst." I confessed, staring up at the ceiling, my heartbeat beginning to return to normal.

"I know, Aims." He sighed, defeatedly. I immediately felt stupid for overreacting and once again, being the problem in our relationship.

My hackles raised instantly at the sound of a feminine sigh on Josh's end of the phone.

"Where are you?" I questioned sharply, not watching my tone. Unease swirled in my belly as I realised, he had lied to me. I knew he had read my message after twelve.

"My flat, Aims." He groaned, I could practically hear him rubbing his temples with annoyance.

"On your own?"

"Are you fucking serious? Amelia, it's ten in the morning, I'm not really down for this interrogation." Bile churned in my stomach at the guilt in his voice.

"FaceTime me." I demanded. "If you're alone, video call me now."

"I'm going back to sleep; this is a fucking joke. If you don't trust me-"

"Now. Josh." My phone beeped. I expected to see the call being converted to a video, instead he had sent an image.

"Are you fucking happy now?" He barked down the phone. I opened the photo of his room from his view on the bed, eager to be proven wrong. As I scanned the image, all seemed to be in order. The pile of his dirty clothes were stacked in their usual place on the chair in the corner, the half-empty cups on top of the unit were present and his bag hung from the door of his wardrobe. I began to lift my phone back to my ear when the strap and cup of a bra that didn't belong to me, hooked onto the edge of the bed, caught my eye.

"I suggest you tell me who you're with, Josh!" My voice sounded strangled.

"What are you on about? You're fucking crazy." He laughed bitterly and my blood boiled.

"I'm not an idiot. Check the edge of your bed. If you don't video call me right now and prove you're alone, we're done."

The line was quiet for a second before he released a defeated sigh, "I guess we're done then."

The phone fell silent.

4

THEO

Squashing myself between our drummer, Finn and bassist, Callum on the sofa in one of the offices of the record company building, I listened intently as our Band Manager, Gary relayed the final details of our European tour.

"To confirm lads, we have fourteen cities booked across four months and the tickets sold out within minutes so we expect the crowds to be wild!" Gary spoke matter-of-factly but the three of us couldn't contain our excited hollering, at the notion that our band was finally reaching the heights we'd always dreamt of. "Keep that energy up lads, it might sound easy but trust me, a quarter of the year on the road can be tough."

Gary proceeded to run us through the logistics of the tour. The travel plans, the cities, the venues and the capacities. "Whilst there'll be a lot of travel on the tour bus, we've tried to book as many hotels as possible to make your time comfortable and a little less chaotic."

"Glad to hear it Gaz, I was concerned I'd be keeping these boys up all night in the bus, if you know what I mean." Sean appeared at the door fashionably late as always.

"With what? Wanking through your tears of loneliness?" Callum needled him. "I think we'll be just fine mate."

"I'm the lead singer of this band; I think you'll find that makes me a bit of a pussy magnet." Sean took a seat in the armchair to the left of us.

"Yeah, yeah, whatever you say, bro." Finn tapped him on his leg in jest. As difficult and off putting as we found Sean to be at times, by God could that boy sing and that made up for almost every arrogant and smarmy joke that he made.

"Right, last order of business. The label thinks it would be great to connect with the fans on a more personal level for this tour, given the height of your success following the film release. We know you all have your individual social media accounts but the label suggested a singular profile which could be used like a tour diary or a blog on the road. We have a few people in mind and will confirm who is chosen next week but wanted to put it on your radar." Gary informed us of the plan.

A lightbulb went off in my brain. "I appreciate you guys are already chatting to some people and I don't want to question your judgement, but can I state the obvious here?" I was met with bewildered looks from the band and Gary, "Amelia."

Gary pondered my words, "hmm, we were looking for someone with more experience," he responded finally, not fully convinced by my statement.

"Without Amelia's blog we wouldn't even be planning this tour, so I think it's safe to say she's qualified." I smiled, trying my best not to flutter my eyelashes at him as I pitched my idea.

Gary paused for a moment, seemingly deep in thought as he mulled over the case I'd presented.

"I hate to admit this, but you're right. She'd bring a good tone and perspective seeing as she's so close with you all. I'll give her a call today."

"I can call her." I interjected too quickly.

"As you're so eager, be my guest. It'll be one thing off my to-do list," Gary laughed, "I'll see you boys soon." He slapped Callum on the back, as he passed by him to the exit.

"Nice work, mate." Finn laughed, looking pointedly at me.

"What do you mean?"

"Getting your crush on the road for four months," Callum nudged my side, "and away from her boyfriend no less, you devil."

"I honestly don't know what you mean, I'm simply helping a friend." I said so innocently they could see my halo shine.

"Maybe it won't be *Sean* wanking through his tears after all." I shoved Finn for his vulgar comment and the four of us chuckled.

"Right, I'm off to call Mils. See you pricks later." I saluted before heading out into the hall.

She picked up on the third ring.

"Finally decided to admit it then?" She barked down the line. Not the greeting I was expecting.

"Whoa, are you okay?" I questioned, my mind reeling over what she could possibly be accusing me of.

"Oh, Theo, it's you. Sorry." She apologised, sounding distant.

"What's wrong, Sunflower?" My voice softened, as she released a shaky breath. "If this is a bad time I'll call you back."

"No, it's fine, just give me some good news." She laughed sadly. I knew the problem was no doubt Josh and it wasn't my place to pry. But good news was certainly something I could help her with.

"Well, I've got a proposition for you." I decided to stop prolonging the suspense as she clearly wasn't in the mood. "As you know the band is going on tour in two months…" I then recited Gary's words to her, practically hearing the cogs turn in her brain as she pieced together what I was asking her.

"As in… I'd come on tour with you?" She questioned, apprehension coating her words.

"Well yeah, you'd have to be at the shows to write about them." I laughed, feeling nervous that I was about to be rejected.

"Alright." She said simply.

For the first time in my life, I didn't know what to say. "Huh?" I asked, dumbly.

"Yeah, why not? Nothing holding me back now." As much as I was overjoyed that she would be joining us, I couldn't allow myself to feel happy when she sounded so distraught.

"It's Josh, isn't it?" I asked the burning question, unable to keep my nose out any longer.

"You know how it is. But this time it really feels over." She choked back a sob and my heart stuttered; I wanted nothing more than to pull her into my arms.

"Oh, Mils. I'm sorry." Morbid curiosity got the better of me, "what happened?"

"Don't worry about it, Theo. It's not important. But I'd love to come on tour with you." She hung up the phone leaving me in the hallway, fifty percent elated for her acceptance and fifty percent disappointed it was under these circumstances.

I made my way back to the boys to give them the news but all I could picture was the watery smile she would be giving me if I was with her right now and I tried my best to bury the need to cuss out Josh for breaking her heart, *again*.

5

AMELIA

Carefully, I folded the clothes into my suitcase. It had been a month since Theo had invited me to join their upcoming tour to write the tour diary. With Christmas coming up, I knew I would be super busy so decided it was best to get as much of the packing complete prior to the festivities.

My friends were over the moon when they heard the news surrounding my work opportunity - even Lilah - who'd recently become my boss along with Zane, although she had complained she was losing her best Marketing Manager and to her brother no less. However, ever the supportive friend, she allowed me the time off regardless. As much as I wanted to go gung-ho into this new venture and attempt being self-employed, I was scared to hand my notice in completely. I needed the safety net of knowing I could return to Moreno Hart Jewellery once this was all over.

It had also been a month since Josh and I had called it quits. Although I had tried to convince myself that it was over for good this time, we had gone on breaks longer than this in the past, so there was still a part of me that believed we would be back together soon.

As the taxi pulled up outside of the destination that Josh had sent me earlier today, a wave of excitement and relief washed over me, eclipsing the stress that had been tying me in knots following the unnecessary argument that had occurred two days previously. Tonight, would be the first time we'd have spoken since – bar the ominous text that I had received.

I thanked the driver and stepped onto the pavement, smoothing my dress that I knew was Josh's favourite. The illuminated sign of the building sparked a memory. Prime – that was the steak place that Josh had been raving about and where it was impossible to get a reservation. He must have gone above and beyond to get us in here!

"Hey boo, you look beautiful," the familiar voice whispered in my ear, as two hands slipped around my waist from behind me. I whipped around to see Josh, dressed smarter than usual. He placed a soft kiss on my lips, butterflies fluttered in my stomach as I melted under his touch.

"Are we okay?"

"Shh, it's behind us now." He reassured, smiling at me, producing a bunch of roses the colour of sunshine.

A knock at my apartment door broke me out of my thoughts. I made my way through and opened it, taken aback by the person standing before me.

Josh.

What was he doing here?

"Wait, please." He stopped the door before I could slam it shut.

"What do you want, Josh?" I sighed, standing my ground.

"To talk, Aims." He pleaded. "Let me explain." I hesitated for a moment before allowing him entry.

We fell into the usual routine. Josh sat in his usual place on my sofa. Reciting the usual apologies, how it 'wasn't how it looked' and I had 'misunderstood' and I allowed it to temporarily stick my broken heart back together again. He handed me a bunch of yellow flowers, identical to the bouquets he had given me each time he fucked up prior and I arranged them in their usual vase. I looked sadly at them, blooming on the windowsill. I should feel happy, but they were just a symbol of his wrongdoing, and they'd eventually wilt, much like his promises.

"I need to tell you something," I confessed sheepishly, returning to him on the leather chair. His eyes narrowed suspiciously. "I'm going away for four months with The Velvet Echoes. They asked me to write a music blog for them and I couldn't turn it down. You know it's my dream to get into music journalism." I braced myself for his reaction, certain an argument was about to ensue. He took a deep breath and rubbed his palms on the legs of his jeans.

"That's amazing news, Amelia," his blue eyes twinkled kindly, "I'm so happy for you."

"It'll be long distance, it'll be hard." I reiterated, surprised by his positive response. Josh had never been overly supportive of my 'little hobby' and I found it difficult to swallow the fact that this time, he may be taking it seriously.

"We'll be fine, we can get through anything, boo." My heart swelled from happiness at this different side of him, maybe the time apart had truly done us some good. I tried with all my might to ignore the nagging voice in the back of my head that wanted to question the validity of his declaration. Perhaps there was another reason he wouldn't mind me not being in town.

He held my hands in his and kissed me on the lips. I allowed myself to give in and get lost in the moment. I had learnt with Josh, when times were good, to roll with it. It wasn't worth raining on our parade, no matter how many questions were left unanswered.

6

THEO

Music blaring through the speakers, sunglasses on, I couldn't wipe the grin from my face as I drove down the road, to reach Amelia's apartment building. Today marked the first day of months living the rockstar life: travelling with the crew, meet and greets with the fans and hearing our lyrics screamed back at us across different European cities! I could hardly contain my anticipation, after what felt like grafting for years in underground establishments, we were finally headlining to sold out audiences of thousands. Once I had collected Amelia, we would be heading to St Pancras station to meet the others and board the Eurostar, ahead of our first gig tomorrow night in Paris.

I rounded the corner to her street and my face fell. She stood outside her building, bags piled on the pavement with an unexpected guest to her side.

Josh.

So much for that breakup then!

I parked alongside the pair and tried to re-paint the smile back on my face, before exiting the car and popping open the boot. Amelia looked incredible, her hair was no longer in braids, the voluminous curls framing her heart shaped face perfectly. She wore baggy jeans and a band t-shirt she had seemingly cut into a crop top. I knew I shouldn't have been checking her out so obviously while her boyfriend was standing in front of me, but it was impossible not to.

"Hey Sunflower, you've packed light!" I glanced down at the bulging suitcase, holdall *and* backpack beside her.

"It's four months, Theo," she laughed. "There's no such thing as overpacking."

"Ah well *I* only brought one bag. I guess if I run out of clothes, you'll have plenty that I can borrow." I tapped Amelia on the shoulder, "we look about the same size." I shot her a wink at the obvious joke, as I towered at least a foot over her, and her boyfriend for that matter, who I could see was scowling in my peripherals before he wrapped a protective arm around Amelia.

"Ah Joshua, I didn't see you there." I greeted sarcastically. "Sorry, there's no spare seat on the train, mate."

Josh opened his mouth to reply before Amelia cut in, "right, shall we go?" She clapped her hands together, trying to dispel the tension. I'd never outright told Amelia my opinions on her partner, but they weren't hard to guess.

"Yep, let's hit the road." I agreed, gesturing towards my car. Amelia bent down to pick up the luggage by her feet. I looked at Josh, expecting his brain to eventually kick into action and retrieve the bags that she was struggling with. When our eyes met, he gave me a blank look, running a hand through his dirty blonde hair and I released a huff.

"Don't worry, mate. I got it." I muttered sarcastically in his direction as I offered a hand to Amelia, taking the suitcase from her and packing it into the car with ease.

Theo 1 - Josh 0

"Come on then, you." I called to her, slamming the boot shut. I looked over just as Josh pulled her face to his and planted a kiss on her lips. I turned away abruptly, not needing to watch the performance.

"I'll miss you, baby." I heard him whisper, glancing up, I saw a flicker of confusion cross Amelia's features, as if she wasn't used to the term of endearment.

"You too." She assured, wrapping her arms around his neck in an embrace. I tried my best to stifle a cough and break up the lovebirds.

Opening the passenger door, I, rather un-subtly, interrupted. "Eurostar won't wait for us, Sunflower."

"Coming!" She laughed, rounding the car and taking a seat. I walked back around to the driver's side, as my hand landed on the handle, Josh spoke.

"Behave yourself." He warned, grabbing my bicep.

I shrugged him off, laughing at his attempt of intimidation. "Right back at you." I said pointedly. Not caring to wait for his response, I joined Amelia in the car and turned on the ignition.

"You can DJ." I said to her, nodding to the sound system.

Once Josh was out of view and she'd finished waving goodbye in his general direction, Amelia turned to me, "what did he say to you?"

I scoffed, "he told me to 'behave myself'." I made finger quotations with one hand, keeping the other on the steering wheel, "like he can fucking talk." I regretted the words the second they left my mouth, looking at Amelia's face, it was clearly a fresh wound. "Sorry, Mils, that didn't come out how I meant it." I ran a hand through my hair.

"You're entitled to your opinion." She shrugged.

"I really wasn't meaning to cause shit, I was only poking fun at him before," I tried to defuse the situation before it escalated. The last thing I wanted was to upset her.

"There's a difference between poking fun and winding him up on purpose. Like him or not, he's my boyfriend." The word felt like a punch to the gut.

Josh 1 - Theo 1

We drove in silence for what felt like an eternity but realistically it had only been a minute or two. Amelia sat scrolling through her phone, whilst I replayed our conversation on a loop, not knowing what to say to break the awkwardness. The music switched to an upbeat song I didn't recognise.

"I came across this band and thought you'd love them." She gushed, looking towards me. The upset in her eyes had disappeared, replaced with their usual warmth.

"Oh- yeah-" I stuttered, "it sounds great. I love the beat."

"I'm surprised you haven't already heard it to be honest, given you're such a fan of my blog." She winked at me in jest. That one small gesture caused relief to spread through my body, the earlier atmosphere dissipating completely. "I posted it on my story last night."

I chuckled, "I'll have to put your notifications on."

"Creep." She slapped my arm and I tried my best to ignore the electric shock that seared at her touch, my body seriously needed to realise that we weren't anything more than friends. "So, Miss Sani, fourteen cities lay ahead of you. What's top of your list?"

"Hmm, well there's some major contenders for the top spot. But I think Lisbon for sure, given I'll be turning thirty-one there. Pastel de natas for breakfast, lunch and dinner!"

"Oh, I didn't realise we would be stealing you away from the City for your birthday!" I made a mental note to buy her a gift.

"Rainy London or beautiful Portugal," she waved her hands like scales, "not much of a competition really!" She laughed.

"Fair point, we'll have to find a way to celebrate in style!"

"Well, whatever you plan, add an extra person on as Josh is going to be visiting then." *Course he is,* I didn't know why I was surprised, they were in a relationship after all. "It'll give you two a chance to bond!" She giggled, noting the displeased look on my face.

I shook my head but a small smile tugged at my lips. "I admire your optimism, Sunflower."

7

AMELIA

Final call for the 15.31 to Paris.

What a sight we must have made, as Theo and I sprinted down the platform towards the first-class carriage, at 3.30pm.

"I told you we should have left earlier." I shouted towards Theo, my heart rate racing.

"We made it didn't we?" He chuckled, bounding along, resembling a pack mule with his rucksack on his back, guitar case in one hand and my holdall in the other.

"Not yet!" I called as the conductor blew the whistle. Our carriage was within touching distance. I shot a panicked look in Theo's direction as he pulled open the door and jumped onboard. He threw out his hand, which I automatically took and yanked me towards him. The door swung shut behind and the train began to move, causing me to lose my footing and stumble into Theo's broad chest. The scent of his signature spicy cologne filled my senses, dizzying me further.

"Told you we'd make it, Sunflower." He winked, looking down at me, with golden eyes. It was in that moment I realised I was essentially wrapped in his arms and jumped backwards to freedom.

"You're lucky, Hart." I said heaving, trying to catch my breath, "now let's go and find the others."

Theo put our luggage into the storage compartments and we made our way through the carriage to our seats. The sound of the band reached us before we saw them.

The three lads were laughing and chatting away over small cans of beer and packets of crisps as we approached their table.

"Ah, decided to show up then?" Finn raised his drink at us in a greeting.

"Don't worry guys, the eye candy has arrived!" Theo looked in my direction, "and I'm not talking about Amelia." He smirked. I released a sigh, oh how I couldn't wait to spend the next four months surrounded by overexcited thirty-year-old boys.

"Hey, Mils," Callum greeted, ignoring Theo's joke. "Tinny?" He held up the lager. I flopped into the unoccupied four-seater and took the can.

"Thanks!"

Theo sat opposite me and cracked open his own beer.

"This is it, lads! The boys are finally on the road." He held his drink out to clink to the rest of the band's, "and Amelia, of course." I tapped my tin to theirs.

Since The Velvet Echoes booked *Accidentally*, I'd only hung out with them as a whole, a handful of times but they were all hilarious and easy to get on with. For this reason, the idea of months on the road with them, seemed a hell of a lot less daunting. I didn't have any siblings of my own but I guessed this was what it would feel like if I were travelling with four brothers.

"Yes, we can't forget our honorary groupie!" Sean joked. Ok, maybe not *four* brothers...

Sean was the only member who I couldn't say I got on with particularly well. As much as the others threw around their fair share of boyish jokes, Sean didn't seem to have an off switch.

"Shut up, Sean." I rolled my eyes playfully.

"You tell him, Millie." Callum added with a chuckle.

After a while of casual conversation, I took out my laptop and began to get myself organised for the tour diary. It was going to be quite full on, having to make sure I took enough photos and wrote up interesting content to keep their fans engaged. To be honest, I couldn't wait though, the thrill of being side of stage watching the band perform live, the surge of adrenaline from the crowds going crazy and being a spokesperson connecting them to the fanbase was a dream come true!

Opening the browser, I began to set up the templates and jot down some content ideas that I knew I wanted to capture.

Individual shots of boys; cool fan signs in the crowd; any time one of the guys pulled a 'we've made it' smile! The list went on.

"Budge up." Theo interrupted my thoughts.

"Huh?" I looked up to see him gesturing with his hands for me to move over. I obliged.

"My turn to share some new music with you!" He scooted beside me, brushed my hair out of the way and popped one of his headphones in my ear.

"I was concentrating!" I pretended to protest, though truth be told, Theo always had good recommendations so I welcomed the interruption.

"Oh shh." He hushed me before pressing play and I let the music flow through me.

We shared his pair of headphones for the remainder of the train journey, taking it in turns to show each other different songs as the world whizzed by around us.

After two and a half hours on the train, crossing country lines, we had arrived at Gare du Nord. I followed the boys through the station towards the exit where we would be meeting their tour bus.

"This is the life!" Callum exclaimed as the large black bus with darkened windows came into view.

"I guess this is us then." Finn laughed, pointing towards the vehicle that was ten times the size of any other car on the road.

We darted between taxis and tourists until we reached the bus door. The driver appeared and introduced himself, letting us into the belly of the beast.

It was out of this world! As we entered, we were greeted by a large kitchen area with a table and TV. Beyond this, were six bunks in pairs of two, lining the walkway, each with their own mini screen and privacy curtain. Lastly, at the back of the vehicle, was a humongous, curved sofa, with a drinks fridge, games system and reclining seats.

"I'm taking this one!" I heard one of the boys shout from behind me. "Cal, you go here."

"Mils, you take the solo one. You don't need a gross guy under you." Theo tapped the top bunk of one of the pairs before jumping up onto the bed opposite. "You can wake up to my pretty face in the morning." He winked.

"I'm a lucky girl." I laughed, hoiking my backpack onto the mattress. We unpacked some basic belongings as we were driven through the city to our hotel for the evening, as the first show tomorrow was in Paris.

We pulled up outside the Shangri-La Hotel, met with a group of fans who were wearing merch and holding signs, who must have heard on the grapevine that the boys would be staying here and were hoping for a glimpse.

"Are they really here to see us?" Theo questioned in amazement, stepping out of the vehicle.

"Yeah, I can't believe it! That girl's wearing a shirt with my face in a heart!" Callum laughed in shock.

Sean and Finn joined us on the pavement and waved towards the crowd, who screamed in response.

"Go on then, don't leave them waiting in suspense." I joked, ushering them over to the hysterical girls.

My heart filled with pride as I watched them signing posters and t-shirts, posing for selfies and chatting animatedly. Taking out my phone, I snapped a few pictures. *This will be perfect for the first diary entry!*

After the impromptu meet and greet, where no person was left unsatisfied, we headed into the lobby and split off to our separate rooms once checked in.

Considering we would only be staying for a couple of nights; the label had clearly spared no expense. I'd never stayed in a hotel room like this before. Marble and gold fixtures were in every corner and I was lucky enough to have a view of the Eiffel Tower. To be honest, I felt a bit guilty considering I was just tagging along and writing some entries. It's not like I would be performing to thousands of people every week! I didn't deserve this.

After exploring every nook and cranny, I sent a picture of the incredible suite to Josh.

SUPERSTAR LIFESTYLE!

Despite not having heard from him all day, I watched the ticks turn blue immediately as he responded with a simple thumbs up.

Involuntarily, my stomach lurched. I could sense
the irritation seeping through the screen and yet I didn't
know what I had done to cause it. Maybe he thought I
was showing off? But I was merely sharing my joy! My
mind flicked back to earlier today, saying goodbye to
Josh and the interaction that he and Theo had.

I saw a different side to Josh. Jealous might be
too far of a stretch but calling me soppy nicknames and
public displays of affection were not his forte, so it felt
disingenuous in the moment. Not to mention Theo's
needling. The pair of them acted like cavemen.

I decided to forward the photo onto the group
chat with my friends as I knew they'd be more supportive
and sitting alone in Paris, that was exactly what I needed!
Seconds passed before the series of enthusiastic messages
began to flood in. I felt the smile spread across my face
as my friends boosted my confidence.

After filling them in with all the details of my day,
it was time to call it a night. I washed my face and
sprawled across the king-size bed, looking up at the
ornate ceiling rose above. A surprising chuckle bubbled
out of my chest. How did I go from standing outside my
apartment in Tooting this morning to a five-star
bedroom on the cusp of finally getting onto the ladder in
the music industry?

8

THEO

The hum of the crowd vibrated through the walls of the arena. Even in the backstage lounge area, far from the main stage, I could hear the fans chanting our name.

I took a deep breath, soaking in the energy of the place. It was kind of a pre-show ritual of mine to have a quiet few minutes by myself before a show.

"Ready, T?" Finn asked, walking through the door, his voice coated with apprehensive enthusiasm as he slapped me on the back.

"You know it." I grinned, my heart was pounding out of my chest but I was too exhilarated to feel nervous. Callum and Sean tumbled into the room, both buzzing with excitement and joined the pair of us, to form a circle.

"I'm so proud to be sharing the stage with you boys tonight. After a hell of a lot of hard graft, we're here in Paris! Let's go out there and fucking smash it!" Finn declared, holding his hand out in front of him.

Instinctively, we all put our hands in too and cheered as we raised them into the air in unison. Following a few quick hugs and slaps on the back, a quick swig of beer and a hair check, we were getting called to the stage.

We were led through the winding corridors of the venue by a staff member, who was smiling and hyping us up. As the decibels of the audience grew louder, my pulse quickened. We reached the side of the stage and I looked around to see if I could spot Amelia. I knew she was busy getting ready for the show, but selfishly, I'd have given anything to hear some words of encouragement from her right now. She'd always been a cheerleader for our band.

I slung the guitar over my body, swallowed a quick sip of water praying I didn't forget any chords. We took our places behind the huge screen, gave each other one last encouraging nod and heard the intro music come to a close.

As the screen lifted to reveal our unlit silhouettes, I began to play the notes to our opening song and the surge of noise from the crowd became deafening. Sean sang the first line and the spotlights focussed on the four of us as we made our way out onto the stage. My eyes darted around the venue, across the thousands of people in the standing area, up to the higher levels. There were flashing lights and smiling faces everywhere shouting our lyrics back at us!

I scanned along the front of the crowd and spotted her. Singing along behind the camera in the space between the barricade and the stage. Amelia looked effortlessly cool with jeans and a tied up TVE band t-shirt. Damn, she made our merch look good!

"Good evening, Pa-ree!" Sean greeted the audience as our first song ended, with a mock French accent. "Are we feeling good tonight?!" The crowd roared in response. "I'll take that as a yes then!" He chuckled, "who wants another?"

I took the signal and began the opening riff. Sean sang the lyrics to our song *What If?* that I had written and I watched as Amelia's ponytail bounced along to the song, she didn't know was about her. I tried to give all areas of the auditorium equal attention but my eyes kept drifting to the girl snapping pictures. Sauntering over to the corner of the stage, I made eye contact with her. She beamed up at me with stars in her eyes. I was certain I had stopped playing, mesmerised by her. After a beat, she pointed the lens towards me, breaking the spell. I winked as the flash went off and began moving to the other side of the stage.

Two hours later, we had reached the encore. "You've been so welcoming, we love you guys! We've got one more for you, so let's hear you sing it at the top of your lungs! See you soon, goodnight!" I shouted into the mic. We played our most popular song, *'Accidentally'* and bid farewell to the night one audience. As we took our final bows, I flicked my eyes to the spot Amelia had occupied for most of the evening. My heart sank when I noticed it was vacant. I had been so engrossed in the last part of the set, that I hadn't seen her leave. I guess she must have gotten enough content and decided to call it a night early.

With one last wave as the lights dimmed, we ran off to the side of the stage. To my surprise, Amelia stood there, grinning from ear to ear, clapping passionately. Subconsciously, I pulled her into my arms and hugged her tightly, lifting her off the floor for a moment. I caught myself, leaning back to see her giggling. "Congrats rockstar, now get off me you're sweaty!"

"As you wish, Sunflower." I released her from my grasp and shook my sweat-drenched hair towards her like a dog. She slapped me playfully on the arm.

"You're gross, Theo." She laughed, turning her attention to the rest of the band. "You were all awesome, the crowd loved you. I can't wait to look through the pictures."

"Thanks, Mils." Callum replied.

"That was electric!" Finn exclaimed, "I want a drink, who's joining?" We all cheered in agreement, walking towards the hallway.

"You guys have fun, see you tomorrow!" Amelia said remaining still, with a look on her face that implied she didn't think the invitation was extended to her.

"Erm, where do you think you're going? You're an integral part of this crew." I strolled back and nudged her shoulder.

"Oh, well, in that case, I'd love to." She shot me a coy smile and I resisted the urge to sling my arm around her as we made our way to the tour bus.

A large group of the band and crew tumbled into the hotel bar when we returned to the Shangri-La, full of adrenaline from the night's activity. A round of beers were ordered and distributed through the crowd. We cheersed our bottles together so hard the bubbles overflowed causing Amelia to lift her drink and attempt to catch the foam with her mouth.

Fuck.

I tried to divert my eyes - and my thoughts for that matter - but I was only human. It was only when I noticed Callum's eyes analysing me that I realised I was staring. He smirked and I kicked him under the table.

We chatted into the early hours of the morning, exchanging details on our favourite signs in the crowd, improvised riffs and fan interactions as we sank countless drinks.

"So, what was your favourite song?" I asked Amelia as we entered the lift ready to call it a night.

"Cor, I hope you don't expect me to stroke your ego every night, Theo or this is going to be a *very* long tour." She rolled her eyes in mock annoyance.

"That's your job: write the blog, take pictures and make me feel good." I counted on my fingers.

"Ah, I must have missed that in the fine print."

"You've gotta be more observant, Mils, or you might miss what's right in front of you." She raised an eyebrow at me as I willed her to read between the lines of my drunken riddle. The elevator bell chimed as we reached the top floor and I gestured for her to lead the way.

"Right missy, I'll catch you in the morning." I said taking the keycard out of my pocket once we reached my room.

"Night, Theo, enjoy your hangover." She tapped me on the back, shooting electricity through my torso.

"Right back at ya, Sunflower." I chuckled, opening my door, trying not to watch as she walked away.

"It was '*What If?*', by the way." Her voice stopped me before I walked through the doorframe, my heart in my throat.

I turned towards her but found she was already walking in the opposite direction. "Mine too." I replied simply under my breath, my voice gravelly with emotion. It took everything in my power not to follow her. Instead, I forced myself into *my* hotel room, closed the door behind me and leant my back against the wood.

The question 'what if?' had long plagued my thoughts ever since I had met Amelia. When Lilah had brought her along to one of our London gigs, a couple of years ago, I was stunned. She was sarcastic and humorous and without blowing my own trumpet, one of the first girls I had chatted up who hadn't immediately taken me up on the offer for a date, which only intrigued me more.

After that meeting, I wrote the song, imagining a world in which we did cross paths again and explore the connection, but it was purely a fantasy. Never in a million years did I imagine I'd be sleeping in a hotel room, a few doors down, yearning to be beside her.

I thought she would always just be my little sister's friend who I occasionally saw and shamelessly flirted with but this past year, getting to know the real her, not just the image I'd created in my head, I was more and more desperate for the lyrics of the song to come to fruition.

9

AMELIA

I startled awake to the noise of someone banging on wood. My eyelids fluttered open and I looked around at the unfamiliar room, trying to get my bearings.

The knocking continued. "Alright, alright." I grumbled, flinging the thick duvet off me and padding, reluctantly, towards the disturbance.

I opened the door to find Theo, hand raised ready to continue his abrupt wake up call.

"*Bonjour*! Wakey wakey, Sunflower." He greeted, a goofy smile spreading across his face.

"God, what time is it?" I rubbed my eyes, I didn't think I'd drunk that much last night but I'd woken up totally disoriented.

He dug his phone out of his back pocket to check, "9:38."

"What?!" I exclaimed, "I never sleep this late!"

"Life on the road I guess." Theo shrugged sarcastically, "it's not late at all, it's barely even morning!" He continued, before leaning a hand on the top of the door frame. I thought about inviting him in but was suddenly all too aware of the skimpy, pink pyjama shorts and camisole I was wearing, quickly crossing my arms over my chest. Theo watched the movement and I felt my cheeks heat.

"Any particular reason for the wakeup call?" I asked.

"The band and I are going to do some touristy things, wanna join?" As much as I appreciated the invitation, I didn't want to fall behind on my first ever diary entry.

"I'd love to, but I've got work to do ahead of the second show I'm afraid. I'm gonna set myself up in front of the window overlooking the Eiffel Tower, I think!" I gestured towards the French doors behind me.

"Come on, it's only day two, you can slack off for a morning." He basically begged.

"Not in my nature I'm afraid," I shook my head, laughing.

"But it's the city of love!" He countered, almost batting his eyelashes.

"Good luck finding it then!" I don't know why he thought that would be the clincher. Romance wasn't exactly on my agenda. "I'll go out with you in Spain." I compromised.

"Alright, you drive a hard bargain, Sani. Have fun on your own." He joked and I rolled my eyes before shoo-ing him out of my doorway.

After a shower and a change of clothes I settled onto the table overlooking the Paris skyline. I'd just logged into the band's Instagram when another knock sounding at my door interrupted me.

"Delivery for the hard worker." Theo announced holding up a croissant and disposable coffee cup. I couldn't help the smile that pulled at my lips.

"Oh, thanks, Theo." I held out my hands for the goods as he passed them over. "You shouldn't have."

"I'm essentially your boss, got to give you some perks!" He winked.

I laughed, "if you say so." The smell of the warm pastry made my stomach grumble.

"We're off now, the bus is due to leave at five, so we'll be back around four. I'll see ya later."

"See you then! Bye." I waved as he made himself scarce.

I sat back down in the chair, staring out at the Parisian view stretching out before me.

Grabbing the camera out of my bag, I plugged the SD card into the slot in my laptop and began sifting through the hundreds of images from the night before.

Pride bloomed in my chest whilst reviewing them. The overwhelmed faces of the fans, the elation in the band's eyes. It was like reliving the night all over again. That was exactly why I wanted to get into the industry in the first place! I flicked onto the next picture and caught my breath.

Theo stood above me on stage, legs spread in a wide stance, hands gripping his guitar, a pick clenched between his teeth and shooting a playful wink just above the camera lens - straight at me.

My heart stuttered at the look in his eye, I knew he was just 'making love to the camera' as they say but I couldn't stop the inappropriate thoughts from flooding into my slightly hungover brain. My thighs involuntarily clenched together as I continued to stare at the image of the sweat-soaked musician for way too long.

Buzzzzz!

My phone vibrated next to me, shaking me out of my far from PG thoughts. I was thankful for the interruption, before I saw the contact that flashed up on the screen.

"Hi Josh." I greeted after picking up, swallowing the guilt that was swirling through me.

"Hey, Aims." He said "how's…where are you again?"

"Paris." I replied, holding back a sigh. I'd literally only been gone for a couple of days and he'd already forgotten.

"Oh yeah, how's Paris?" He sounded distant, like he didn't overly care for the answer.

"Good thanks! The show was amazing, I'm just working at the moment, I've got to get the first diary entry uploaded. How're you?"

"Hmm," he hummed, clearly not listening as he failed to answer my question. "Have you booked my plane by the way?"

I wracked my brain trying to remember what he was referring to. "What plane?"

He sighed, "Ugh, the plane to Lisbon obviously? For your birthday?" His bitter tone got my back up.

"I thought *you* were booking it, Josh?" I emphasised.

"For fuck's sake. Do I have to do everything?!" I could practically hear him throwing his hands up in exasperation. Anger bubbled beneath the surface at his selfish attitude. It was for *my* birthday. Why should *I* have to organise it? "Fine. What are the dates again?" He relented. I told him the information for the umpteenth time, biting my tongue to avoid any confrontation. The last thing I wanted was to argue from different countries. "Leave it with me."

"I really appreciate it. I'm super busy with all the band stuff, so thank you." I responded, trying to keep the peace.

"Oh yeah?" His voice dripped with sarcasm.

"What?"

"Well, you're essentially on a glorified holiday with four men." He laughed bitterly. "I hope you're not *that* busy."

The familiar rage flowed through me at the implication. Of course Josh didn't understand the work I was doing. I was foolish for thinking his attitude had changed the day I told him about the tour.

I took a deep breath. "Well, I have to go now, Josh. I'll see you in Lisbon in a few weeks." He mumbled his own version of a goodbye and hung up the call.

Placing the phone beside my laptop I wiggled the mouse, waking up the system only to be jump scared by the damn picture of Theo that sparked the concoction of emotions in the first place.

Angrily, I closed the photo gallery, groaning under my breath, deciding it was safer to focus on the written content of the post first.

Several hours later, after completing my work for the day and packing away my belongings, it was time to head to the next city.

I took a seat on the comfy sofa at the back of the bus, settling in with my laptop to browse the internet when Theo bounded over and took a seat to my side.

"How was the sightseeing? Did you soak in everything Paris had to offer?" I asked, interested in what the boys had gotten up to over the afternoon whilst I was holed up in my hotel room.

"Yeah, it was great! We found there was an exhibition at the Grand Palais for seventies rock so checked that out, grabbed some food to go and walked to the Eiffel Tower. Took an obligatory picture of us and meandered back!" His grin was infectious. "Here." He held out his phone with the group photo as evidence.

"Very sweet!" I laughed, looking at the four boys, arms around each other, smiling like Cheshire cats. "Can you send that to me?"

"One for your personal collection?" He smirked. I felt my cheeks warm from the comment, as if I didn't already have enough photos of him to scramble my senses.

"For the blog you idiot!"

"Yeah, yeah, if you say so." He tapped me on the shoulder before sending the image to my phone, "enjoy, Sunflower."

After saving the photo, I subconsciously flicked to Josh's chat. It had become a bit of a habit to check that I hadn't missed a message or had definitely sent the last one when I hadn't heard from him for a while. As suspected: radio silence.

"What's Joshua up to then?" Theo enquired, clearly watching me.

"Beats me." I huffed, knowing that I didn't have to pretend around him. "Although I'm sure you knew that answer, spying over my shoulder." I nudged.

"Oh-uh-" he stuttered, I enjoyed seeing him speechless for once.

"You should be careful, you might have seen something you didn't want to." I giggled, knowing full well my conversations with Josh were plainer than vanilla.

"I'm sure anything he would send, wouldn't intimidate me." He smirked, his quick wit returning once again. I didn't know how to respond and shook my head in disbelief. "No seriously though, are things okay?"

I stilled for a moment. I knew that I could be honest with Theo but somehow saying it out loud was like I was admitting it to myself too. However, looking at

Theo's warm, kind eyes, I decided to divulge the true details.

"They're okay at best." I answered simply. He sobered, the earlier cheeky chappy replaced with genuine care. "Not a great deal has changed since we got back together at Christmas. I thought maybe some time apart, with me on the road would do us some good, but old habits die hard, I guess."

"I'm sorry, Mils, that's shit." He paused, as if trying to find the right words to say, "what do you think he's busy doing?" I knew what he was implying and fought against my mind not to wander there.

"I don't need to keep tabs on his whereabouts," I snapped harsher than I intended to. I knew Theo was only trying to be a friend. "Anyway, how's your love life? Considering you're so interested in mine!" I laughed.

"Next to non-existent."

"Oh, come on, the famous lothario, Theo Hart, you've got quite the reputation!" I winked and watched as he recoiled into himself slightly at my statement.

"Christ, I'm sure they're exaggerated stories." He replied awkwardly, rubbing his neck with his hand.

"I've heard all about your shag pad from Lilah. Wasn't that the reason you recommended her as a Personal Assistant to Zane in the first place, to get your privacy back?"

"I don't kiss and tell, Sunflower." He stretched out, resting his arms on the back of the sofa, one of them falling behind me. I tried not to focus on how close he was to me, how I could feel his bicep against my hair and smell his cologne. The way it would have been so easy for him to wrap his arm around my shoulders instead of draping it over the seat. "I'll admit, I've enjoyed myself in the past but I'm seeking deeper connections these days."

I hummed in agreement, unsure what to respond as a wave of unexpected jealousy crashed in my stomach. I shouldn't feel anything about Theo being with other women.

Sort yourself out, Amelia! You must be ovulating. My hormones had to be the only answer to the rollercoaster of emotions I had experienced today!

10

THEO

For the remainder of the drive from Paris, the four of us took it in turns to battle each other on the games console whilst Amelia lounged on the sofa, laughing at the immature insults we hurled at each other when ever one of us lost. As the time rolled into the early hours, the group began to drop like flies until just Finn and I remained.

"I'm gonna head to bed, don't stay up too late!" Finn joked, finishing the beer he was drinking.

"Just going to wrap this up quickly, then I'm going to sleep too," I responded. I was midway through scrawling some notes for a new song and I had to get it out before I forgot it completely.

"Nice, sure we'll be hearing it soon no doubt. Guess you've got lots of things to write about now Amelia's with us." Finn joked as I silently cursed him to shut up, knowing she was only a few metres away in her bunk, potentially still awake, hearing every word. He lowered his voice, "have you admitted your feelings to her yet?"

"Don't know what you're talking about," I replied innocently. Although it was glaringly obvious, I'd never confirmed it to the boys. Finn chuckled before heading towards the bunks. "She got back with Josh before Paris, so doesn't matter anyway."

Finn turned back to me, "that's shit mate." He threw me a sympathetic smile and disappeared back to his bunk leaving me alone with my thoughts.

****

Racing along the corridor to Amelia's room, I was concerned as I hadn't heard from her since we checked in at 7am. We were due to leave the hotel in around twenty minutes to get to the venue of tonight's show. As I approached her door, the unmistakable sound of her being sick echoed into the hallway. Tentatively I knocked on the wood, as I heard the toilet flush.

"Let me in, Mils." I implored, certain she would be feeling too embarrassed to open the door.

"No way, I'm so gross. You're not coming in here!" She whined weakly back.

"Don't be stupid, nothing I haven't seen before."

"You haven't seen *me* being sick before." She countered, although I could hear her footsteps lingering by the entranceway.

"First time for everything, Sunflower." I persuaded. With that, she cracked the door open slightly. I was taken aback by how unwell she looked. Dark circles, hair unkempt and tears welling in her eyes as she stood leaning against the frame.

"Don't say I didn't warn you." She smiled meekly. Without thinking I reached out towards her feeling her forehead with the back of my hand.

"Jesus, you're burning up, Mils!" She ducked away from me slightly and shrugged.

"I'll be alright, maybe it was the travelling."

"Oh no, didn't you think you should mention you suffer with travel sickness before coming on tour?" I joked, rolling my eyes.

"Shut u-" Her eyes widened and she covered her mouth before diving towards the bathroom once again. I followed her in as she knelt over the toilet, without thinking, scraping her hair into a makeshift ponytail as she expelled the contents of her stomach. "I'm so sorry." She croaked between breaths.

"Shh." I hushed her, rubbing soothing circles on her back as she vomited again. "It's okay." After a further minute she sat back and wiped under her eyes before reaching up and flushing.

"God, I feel awful." Her voice sounded hoarse and I retrieved a bottle of water from beside the sink. "Thanks." She took a swig, sweat coated her brow, colour drained from her face, she looked exhausted.

"You look terrible."

"Thanks, Theo. I can see why your love life's in shambles with those compliments." I chuckled, trust Amelia to take the piss after I'd just witnessed her puking her guts up. I would've ribbed her back if I wasn't so concerned. Panic filled her eyes. "What time is it?" She questioned. I took out my phone to check.

"Five to six." I answered simply.

"Shit! Theo, you're going to be late. Go ahead without me and I'll catch you up!" She began to peel herself up off the floor as quickly as she could, which at this moment in time, was at a snail's pace. I couldn't help the laugh from bursting out of my chest. "What?"

"Amelia, you're obviously not coming." I helped her to stand fully upright. "Look at you, you're so unwell. You need to rest." I began to guide her towards her bed, clearing the pile of belongings she must have been in the middle of unpacking.

She slowly sat down and leant against the pillows I had stacked for her. "How am I going to write about a show that I didn't attend?" She pouted, looking too adorable for someone so ill.

"Well, lucky for you, you've got a man on the inside." I smirked; she furrowed her brow. "Me, I'll be right in the thick of the action. I can bring you notes later!"

"Well, you'll be biased, Theo. It will all be about the fit guitarist." She rolled her eyes, but I couldn't help the smile from spreading across my face.

"Fit guitarist hey?" I asked.

"They're your words, Theo. Not mine."

"Not yet they're not." I shot her a wink and she groaned, clearly over my flirting for one afternoon. "Anyway, I can tell I'm making you nauseous again, so I'll leave you to recover." I pulled back the cover and tucked her in, flicking the TV on and finding *The Office US* on Netflix, as I knew it was one of her comfort shows. "Right, you get some rest. And I'll be back after the show." I turned to say goodbye only to find Amelia's eyes shut as she had already drifted off to sleep.

A small smile tugged at my lips as I tiptoed towards the exit of her room and turned the big light off. I hoped she would make a recovery before tomorrow and selfishly I was going to miss looking for her pretty face in the crowd tonight.

11

AMELIA

Lying in bed half asleep, wrapped up in a cloudlike duvet, I watched my favourite episode of the American comedy for the hundredth time. My stomach was empty and my whole body felt as if I had been hit by a car, but I supposed there were worse places to be cooped up in bed feeling sorry for myself. I decided to let myself wallow in self-pity, consumed by the guilt of missing the first show in the second city. Although I was certain Theo wouldn't have let me leave this room even if I tried. My belly rumbled, reminding me of how hungry I was. I knew it was risky, but I always craved the greasiest, cheesiest pizza after throwing up. However, I had no idea where to source one from in Madrid at twelve at night and I was certain room service had stopped running by now.

The beep of my door unlocking startled me, I pulled the covers up around my body and froze feeling immediately vulnerable. Despite my speedy recovery, it didn't seem my fight or flight was working.

"Delivery." Theo's voice called as he entered my room.

"God, you scared the shit out of me." I clutched my chest, panting. The fear subsided as the scent of hot food emanated into the room.

"Sorry, Sunflower. I took your spare keycard before the show." He closed the door behind him and walked over to the bed, holding out a takeaway box.

"I should be concerned that you're just letting yourself into my room Theo, but if that's what I think it is-"

"I know, I know, pizza's a weird choice." He put the delicious smelling box on the bed and sat beside me, my stomach growled louder. "But the only thing I want after chucking my guts up is a margherita." He flipped open the lid to reveal the most appetising looking midnight snack.

"You read my mind!" The words had barely left my mouth before I shovelled a slice in. "This is amazing!" I stopped, looking at him. "Are you really just going to watch me eat this on my own?"

"Well, I was planning to share it with you but the way you were looking at it, I didn't want to come between you guys. I'm feeling like a third wheel." He laughed, scrubbing his stubble with his hand. I took him in for a second, his hair was messed up from the gig, a distressed black t-shirt clung to his broad frame and his aftershave mixed with the post-show musk was almost as appealing as the pizza.

"Well let's make this a throuple then," I joked, holding out a slice. "Tuck in!"

We began to chow down on the food. "I take it you're feeling better then?" He asked, wiping the corner of his mouth with a napkin he must have brought in with the box.

"Much better now thanks." I replied, feeling invigorated. "How was the concert? I was gutted to miss it!"

"It was good. Crowd was great and the guitarist looked extra fit." He nudged my arm with his elbow. "I'd regret missing that too." I paused for a moment. Could he *actually* read my mind?!

"Would you describe Callum as a guitarist? I think of him more of a bassist?" I probed, giggling.

"Very good, Sani." He rolled his eyes, "think yourself a joker, do ya?"

"It must be your influence." I laughed, my previous sickness bug all but forgotten. "No after show drinks tonight then?"

"Ah the boys have gone out but the idea of a greasy pizza was too enticing and I'd feel bad leaving Sick Note here on her own." He pointed to me. A surprising rush of elation coursed through me at the idea that he had left his friends and the prospect of exploring a new town - and new women - to look after me.

We finished the food, whilst binging several episodes of the show and chatting mindlessly into the early hours of the morning. I yawned, rubbing my eyes, we had both sunk against the headboard and I was beginning to feel fatigued.

I leant my head against his shoulder and smiled as he returned the gesture, leaning his cheek against my hair. I couldn't remember the last time someone had cared for me like this, I usually tried to hold myself together when I was feeling unwell so as not to inconvenience anyone or get behind on work but being able to fully switch off my brain for the past few hours had done wonders and I felt as good as new.

"Thank you for today." I sighed.

"No need to thank me, Sunflower." He responded.

"I really appreciate all you've done, though." I implored. We sat in silence for a minute. My words hung in the air as a warm feeling spread across my chest. I hadn't felt this in a long, long time and it was hard to pinpoint its root. A niggling voice in the back of my head told me I was acting inappropriately but at that moment I was certain of Theo and I's relationship. "You're such a good friend to me."

12

THEO

Friend.

It was incredible how one word could feel like a gut punch. I shouldn't be surprised. She has a boyfriend, what more would I be? But the reminder knocked me momentarily for six.

I listened to her steady breaths and watched the gentle rise and fall of her chest as she slept peacefully, it was clear why my thoughts had gotten carried away today. Snuggled up on the hotel bed, laughing together, eating dinner together, it felt so natural to be with her. The way she had fallen asleep with her head on my chest caused my heart to swell. I knew I needed to get out of there, it would be too easy to stay with her body curled up to mine but it would be crossing the line. I didn't give a shit about Josh's feelings but if we woke up tangled together, I knew Amelia would carry the guilt with her and that wasn't something I wanted to encourage – no matter how much it pained me to leave.

I began to slowly shuffle out from underneath the covers so as not to disturb her. Amelia whined as I disrupted her sleep and her fingers grabbed at my t-shirt. A small chuckle rumbled in my chest and I fought against every urge to stay yet again. I untangled her hands from the fabric and she stretched before turning away from me and snuggling deeper into the duvet.

Walking quietly across the room, I picked up the empty pizza box and made my way to the door. As I opened it, I turned back to steal one more look at Amelia sleeping soundly in the bed. I paused for longer than necessary almost as if I was willing her to wake up and beg me to stay.

Come on man, time to go.

I shut the door tentatively and made my way back down the hall towards my empty room. I settled into my own bed and flicked through social media, liking posts from fans who had attended the gig tonight. Once I'd seen more photos of my face than I cared to see, I began swiping through people's stories. Lilah's appeared showing a photo of Zane surrounded by numerous slices of cake with the text 'cake tasting' over the top. Wedding cake tasting I presumed!

"I hope you don't find this odd, but seeing as you're the only family Delilah has, I felt it was my duty to ask for your permission." Zane said, handing me a beer, with a flicker of nervous energy.

"Permission for what, man? Bit late for that, isn't it?" I laughed, unsure where this was going. He had invited me over to his and Lilah's house on a random Tuesday when Lilah was at a gym class and as much as I loved a spontaneous catch up with my boy, I was unclear on the real reason as to why he had asked me over so out of the blue.

Zane rolled his eyes before his stoic expression returned. "You've always been so supportive of us, even when you didn't have to be. Never gave me shit for dating your little sister or lying to you about it for that matter. As I told you a year ago, I can't live without her and I'd be honoured if you'd allow me to ask for her hand in marriage."

I was shocked by the question then immediately overcome with emotion. Lilah and I's father had been out of the picture since we were kids and our mother, Esmerelda, had passed away, so we really were all each other had left in the world. To think that Zane respected me this much to ask for my blessing meant more than I could comprehend.

"Welcome to the family, brother."

I messaged Lilah subtly persuading her to pick the chocolate option - my favourite - and locked my phone. I'd barely put it down before it started to vibrate.

"Hey man! You're up late?" I asked Zane, checking the clock and realising it would be gone 1am back in the UK.

"Between wedding planning and running a business, sleep is pretty limited at the moment." He laughed. "How's Madrid?"

"Good! Well, I've not seen much of it yet to be honest, but the show was awesome."

"Surprised you're not out with a horde of girls." He chuckled and I rolled my eyes.

"Well, I *was* with a girl," I debated whether to mention anything to Zane given his relationship with Lilah, one of her best friends, "but that's complicated."

"So, are you going to tell me who or not? I'm not digging for information."

"Jesus, I just stopped to breathe." I paused, Zane possessed an array of great skills but one he lacked was patience! It was now or never. "It's Amelia."

"Hmm, figures." Zane said simply, like it was the obvious answer. "She has a boyfriend, you know?" I could hear his smirk down the line, his words coated in sarcasm.

"Yes, I'm well aware. Hence the complications!" I flung my free hand up in the air in annoyance as if he could see me. "Not hearing many words of wisdom from you, mate." I rubbed my hand over my eyes.

"Look, I don't know what's happened between you two but-"

"No-no, nothing's happened." I sighed, quick to prove my innocence.

"Well then, you're golden. You're allowed to be her friend, T." His voice softened as he realised my inner turmoil.

"I know, it's just-"

"Complicated." Zane cut in repeating my earlier words.

"Hmm," I hummed, "anyway what's your cake choice?" I not so subtly changed the subject. We chatted for a further ten minutes before calling it for the night. I turned on the TV and drifted off to episodes of dramatic Spanish soap operas that I didn't understand, letting my tiredness pull me into sleep.

The next morning, I found a spot on the sofa and began to practice some riffs on my guitar, seeing which new melody stuck to the lyrics I had written on the bus. I had found myself inspired of late. A knock on my door abruptly ended the session.

Amelia stood in the hallway, looking worlds away from the sick patient I looked after twenty-four hours ago. Her tight curls fell around her shoulders, framing her face.

"Well, this is awkward. One of us is going to have to change." She joked, pointing between us. We both stood there wearing band merch and blue jeans.

"No chance, Sunflower. Looks like we're twinning today." I winked, "to what do I owe the pleasure of your visit?"

"I'm sick of hotel rooms or more specifically hotel room bathrooms, I want to see the city!" She gushed, "wanna join me?"

I looked around the dull room, pretending to consider my answer. "I suppose I can spare a few hours." I jested.

"Great! Are you ready now?" Her brown eyes blinked up at me eagerly, how could I say no to her?

"Give me two minutes. Come in." I gestured for her to enter and she bounded past me.

"Someone's clearly feeling a lot better!" I smiled whilst retrieving my trainers from beside the wardrobe.

"Yeah, I slept like a baby last night, I don't even remember falling asleep." A strange feeling twisted in my chest at how different last night seemed to be for the both of us. "Jesus, your room is a tip!" She scoffed, breaking me out of my uncomfortable thoughts.

"It's not that bad." I defended, although admittedly, it looked as if a bomb had gone off. "It's only temporary." I chuckled, watching as she picked up one of the shirts which had been carelessly thrown on the sofa.

"I love this band!" Amelia announced, holding up my Paper Sunsets top from their first ever tour. "This shirt is so cool; I can never find their old merch anywhere!"

"You're a woman of taste," I complimented. "I meant what I said when I picked you up, I'm more than happy for you to share my clothes, Mils." In fact, there was a very large part of me that longed to see her in my shirts.

"I'll bear that in mind." Amelia chuckled, folding the shirt neatly and placing it on the chair with much more care than I had done previously. "Hurry up, let's go!"

The rest of the band wanted the day off after partying well into the early hours and were all now nursing mighty hangovers leaving Amelia and I to explore alone. The two of us wandered through the streets of Madrid, dipping into local shops to peruse the items and pick up souvenirs. Ultimately, we ended in a music shop, thumbing through the vinyls to see if we could find any hidden gems.

"Oh wow, Theo, have you seen this?" Amelia called from across the row of boxes, filled with records. I glanced towards her as she held up an intricately designed sleeve.

"Is that the first pressing of The Undergrounds' debut album?" I loved that band; they reminded me of my mum as she played them all the time when Lilah and I were children. It would appear that Amelia appreciated them just as much as me from the look on her face. "How much is it?"

"Errr," she flipped it over and pulled an exaggerated worried look, "six-fifty."

"Keep a hold of it, that's mine now." I said with a smile as I rounded the row of vinyls I had been sifting through to approach her.

"Alright money bags, lunch is on you then." She shot me a wink as I took the record from her hands and began walking to the counter.

It was still strange for me to splash the cash frivolously. I'd always worked hard for the pennies and never had that much excess to splurge on luxuries but when the band took off, my bank balance rose with it and I was trying my best to enjoy the fruits of my labour!

"Of course, Sunflower."

A couple of hours later, after exhausting ourselves shopping in the various lanes of the city, we came across a tapas bar and decided it was time for some sustenance.

We ordered a selection of local small plates which had been recommended by the waiter and a jug of sangria.

"So, you need to fill me in on all the details from last night as I need to write the post asap!" She demanded, popping an olive in her mouth and opening the notes app on her phone, like a modern journalist.

"Put the phone away, your work here is done!" I was met with a confused look.

"Theo, I really need to get this info, I'm running out of time." She begged, stress and worry beginning to creep into her beautiful brown eyes.

"Calm down, cutie." I dug out my notebook, thumbing the pages until I found the one covered in my scruffy handwriting, outlining the main newsworthy points of the evening; the person that Sean had had a hilarious exchange with between songs; the explicit sign with a picture of a girl's boobs with the tagline 'ROOM 132 – HOTEL MADRID – IF YOU WANNA SEE MORE'; and the extended drum solo that Finn played towards the end of the set much to the audience's – and our – amazement! I ripped it out before handing it over, "here you go."

She took it from me and scanned the words animatedly, "are you serious, Theo? This is amazing! Thank you so so much." The light returned to her eyes and a smile formed so wide, I was certain it could have knocked me off my chair from being so dazzling.

I held my glass out towards her and she returned the gesture. "Now you can relax, enjoy Madrid and this wonderful company."

13

AMELIA

"Happy birthday!" My friends chorused through my device on FaceTime.

"What are your plans, gal?" Lilah asked jovially, "you're in Lisbon now, how fun!" She was right, I was so excited to be here and it was the place I had been looking forward to visiting the most! But we had arrived late last night so I hadn't had a chance to explore just yet. I was *so* ready to leave the hotel, meet Josh and see everything that this beautiful place had to offer!

"Josh should be due to land any minute and then we're straight out to grab a pastel de nata and see the sights!"

"Sounds lovely, do you have a show tonight?" Verity asked, her blue eyes sparkling with interest.

"No, not today, so I've got the whole day free! Back to business tomorrow." I replied, "Jake, you're quieter than usual? What's wrong?" I asked, knowing how much my best friend enjoyed the sound of his own voice.

"My gift to you is silence on your relationship. I will not offer any opinion or say any snarky remarks for the next twenty-four hours." He responded, deadpanned.

"You just did," I dug at him, laughing and rolling my eyes. Jake meant well and I loved him for looking out for me but sometimes the negative comments on my relationship with Josh were not necessary, so I appreciated that today of all days, he was keeping his opinions to himself.

"Trust me, I could say *a lot* worse," Jake continued holding his hand up, "but I won't, cos it's your birthday."

"Thank you very much, Jake." I giggled.

"Most important question, how's Theo?" He took me by surprise and I felt my face warm with embarrassment. There was no reason for the innocent question to knock me off guard but with three pairs of eyes boring into me digitally, especially given the fact one of them was Theo's sister, I realised I had taken too long to respond.

I cleared my throat, "ye-yeah he's great!" I played with one of my ringlets.

"Cor, I'm jealous of you getting to spend so many nights alone with him!"

"That's my brother you're talking about, gross!" I could tell Lilah wanted to slap his arm through the screen.

"You're jealous of all our boyfriends, babe." Verity chimed in, who was no stranger to people gawking over her Hollywood superstar partner.

"He's not my boyfriend!" I protested, slightly firmer than I intended. My phone began to beep with an incoming call from my *actual* boyfriend. "Sorry, I've got to go, Josh is calling me. He must have landed, speak soon!"

"Love you."

"Have a great day!

"Send pics!" They spoke over each other as I ended their call and accepted Josh's.

"Happy birthday, Aims." He greeted. A guilty tone clung to his words.

"Thanks! Where are you? Shall I send a car?" I questioned, assuming he was in the same country as me, trying to remain positive despite the gnawing feeling in my stomach.

"Look, Aims, the thing is," he started and my heart sank immediately, "I tried to book a flight, I really did but by the time I looked it up there were no seats available."

The usual feeling of anger began to rage inside of me before a stronger emotion won out. I tried my best to fight back the tears that were pooling in my eyes.

"Okay, well that's shit but it is what it is I guess." I responded, trying to keep my voice level, I didn't want this conversation to devolve into a full-blown argument.

"I'm sorry." He apologised, surprising me, "but this is exactly why I said you should have booked it. You know how forgetful I am!"

I sniffled, "I know, sorry, don't worry about it." I could feel the sob in my chest, "I've got to go." I heard him begin to speak again but couldn't bear to hear more excuses and hung up the phone.

Instantly, I dissolved into floods of tears, my chest heaving as the heartbreak and disappointment consumed me. It was my birthday for God's sake, this was a low blow even for Josh! Despite all his previous shortcomings, he had always made me feel special on this day in the past.

Between my whimpers, I heard a rap at my hotel room door. For a split second, I fooled myself that it was Josh and he had been pranking me all along; however, I instead found Theo on the other side.

"¡*Hola!* Happy birthd-" He began, holding out a pastel de nata with a single unlit candle stabbed into the set custard, "what's wrong?!" He sobered, catching sight of my tear-stained face and bloodshot eyes. The genuine concern for my wellbeing only made me cry harder.

"He's not coming," I managed through my tears as Theo pulled me in for an all-encompassing hug and I sank against his chest.

"I'm sorry, Mila." He whispered.

After a few minutes of standing in Theo's arms, I had calmed down. "Some birthday this is." I laughed sadly. "Solo plans for me!"

He held me at arm's length. "Sunflower, you're not spending your birthday alone. Give me thirty minutes and I'll be back with an extravaganza planned." His goofy grin pulled an unexpected smile from me and I wiped the stray tears from my face before giving him a nod.

I padded back into my room, checking my phone. No message from Josh. No surprise there. I reapplied some makeup to look presentable again and waited for Theo to return. It's amazing how he had done more for me in the past five minutes than Josh had all morning.

14

THEO

What a fucking prick!

The heartbreak on Amelia's face was etched into my brain as I did some panicked Googling of 'fun things to do in Lisbon on your birthday'.

I noted down a few activities and spots of interest on my phone and hurried back to pep up the birthday girl.

She let me in and I was pleased to see that she was in better spirits than before. As usual, she looked effortlessly cool and drop-dead gorgeous. Today she wore her hair half up, large silver hoop earrings and a dark gloss across her full lips.

"Okay, Sunflower, surprise number one!" Hiding one of my hands behind my back as she gave me an inquisitive look. "Not that you don't already look amazing, but I knew you liked this. So, for one day only, you get to wear my favourite piece of merch." I held out the Paper Sunsets vintage tee, that she had commented on previously, towards her.

"No way, really?" She took it from my hand and looked at it as if it was a priceless artefact. "Is it clean?" She quirked an eyebrow, beginning to take off her jacket.

"Washed it especially for ya." I winked.

"Turn around then, I don't want any prying eyes."

I gulped and did as I was told, boring a hole into the white wall of her bedroom, fighting every urge to turn around as I heard her remove her top and replace it with mine. I could only imagine how breathtaking she'd look lifting her shirt above her head, the curve of her waist, the swell of her breasts.

"Ready!" She exclaimed, disrupting my thoughts. I released a breath. Turning back to see Amelia in a pair of jeans with my t-shirt tied in a knot, the orange material complemented her dark skin. A sliver of her toned midriff peeked out from above the hem of her trousers. I dragged my gaze leisurely up to her face, to be met with a knowing smile. Although she didn't mention it, I had definitely been caught red-handed checking her out. But looking like that, dressed in *my* clothes, who could blame me?

"Suits you." I complimented simply after clearing my throat. I clapped my hands together and let my grin spread across my face. "Let the birthday bonanza begin!"

The first activity on my hastily planned day of surprises was a tram ride to a wine bar. We walked up one of the ridiculously steep hills towards one of the stops, heaving for breath as we reached the peak.

Almost instantly, a yellow tram car came hurtling down the road towards us. We jumped on and I bought our tickets, before finding a seat by the window. As the city began to pass us by, I couldn't help but view it from Amelia's point of view. Her expression resembled an excited child on Christmas morning and her eyes glowed with wonderment as she took in the architecture and beauty of the place.

Josh was a fucking idiot for letting her down again. How he couldn't see how special she was, was beyond me.

"This is us." I said, gesturing for Amelia to exit the tram.

We walked a few minutes as I followed the map on my phone leading me towards our destination.

Finally, we reached an ornately tiled building on the corner of the street. I led Amelia through the doorway and down a set of stairs, into the cellar. A waiter met us when we reached the bottom and took us to a dark wooden table in the middle of the room. I had called ahead and booked out the entire venue to ensure we had some time alone. The perks of being in a famous band!

A charcuterie board of Spanish meats and cheese was set up with four empty wine glasses lined up on either side.

"Take a guess, Sunflower." I suggested, pulling out her chair before she slid onto it.

"Wine tasting?!" She exclaimed, as I took a seat opposite her.

"Not much gets past you!" I winked.

"Not just a pretty face," she laughed, picking up a slice of Manchego. I took a moment to take her in. It was the middle of the day but underground, in the darkness of the bar, the candlelight from the jar on the table, illuminated in a way that accentuated her beauty to other heights.

"Up first is our delicious light white wine from Catalonia. It has a zesty initial taste with a citrus finish. I hope you enjoy it." The waiter poured us a glass each and left.

I took a sip, swilling it around my mouth before swallowing, doing my best to appear like a real wine connoisseur to keep up appearances.

"I don't know anything about wine tasting!" She stage-whispered across the table with a glint in her eye.

"Me neither, Sunflower." I confessed, "but I know how to drink it." I cheersed her glass and took a large gulp. "Happy birthday, Amelia."

"Thank you and thanks for everything you're doing today. I really appreciate it!" She was looking at me as if I'd hung the moon yet I felt it was the bare minimum she deserved.

"Oh, we're just getting started!" I promised.

We finished our glasses and the waiter reappeared, introducing the bottle of red he had brought to the table, which was next on our list to try.

"How are you enjoying tour life so far?" I asked
her, snacking on the meat selection after the glasses had
been refilled.

"It's so fun, I'm loving it." She replied.
"Although it's exhausting and I'm only watching! I can't
imagine what it's like for you guys on stage. What
number are we at now?"

"Tomorrow will be show number seven." I
informed, tasting the drink. We were in the third city of
our European tour and although we had played multiple
shows a week in different venues, I still felt the same
amount of energy and enthusiasm at each one. I
wondered if I would hold onto this giddy feeling for the
remainder of my career or if there would ever be a point
when playing to thousands of people felt as normal as
serving drinks at The Gilded Cage. "This one is my
favourite so far!"

"The wine or the city?" Amelia giggled, finishing
her second glass.

"Yet to be determined." I flirted shamelessly. The
wine bolstering my confidence. I couldn't tell her this was
my favourite *day* ever, spending it solely with her and
soaking in all her brilliance.

Over the next hour and a half, we completed our
tour of the Spanish vineyards from the comfort of our
table and polished off the platter. Feeling half cut, I
directed Amelia to the next location of our Portuguese
adventure.

As we walked beside each other, I felt the
electricity emanating between us. Our hands brushed

ever so slightly and I tried to keep my distance but I was drawn to her like a magnet. Like a north and south pole inexplicably thrust together, with no way of fighting the inevitable.

"Now I hope you like karaoke!" I declared, holding my arms out towards the bar which had a lit-up neon sign in the window.

"This is random." She stated, though her eyes shone with amusement

"Well, you like music." I shrugged.

"Yeah, listening to it, not performing it." She responded, appearing bashful. What I had noticed about Amelia, was for all her strong and confident exterior, she was incredibly vulnerable and afraid of standing out.

"Time to switch it up. You perform and *I'll* listen for a change." I smirked, "come on, it'll be fun." I tugged at the corner of her jacket, leading her into the dive bar.

"They must have some Velvet Echoes in here." Amelia said, scrolling through the song selection menu. I poured us two pints of beer from the jug I had bought on the way in.

"Oh, come on! Don't you hear enough of that?" I rolled my eyes, taking a sip of my drink, secretly feeling pleasure at the thought that she wanted one of my songs to perform for the first time.

"Umm, yeah so I know the words!" She laughed, "less chance of embarrassing myself."

"It's only me, Sunflower. No judgement here." I reassured her as we were in a private soundproof booth.

"Bingo!" She exclaimed, removing her jacket, as I heard the instrumental version of our most popular song begin to play through the speakers and the lyrics appear onscreen.

I sat back against the seat cushions, folding my ankle over my knee and stretching my arms out along the top of the sofa. I was mesmerised. She sang along, confidence blooming, not missing a single word as she twirled around with no inhibitions. As I watched her singing *my* lyrics, swaying her hips in time to *my* melody and wearing *my* t-shirt, I felt a stir in my lower abdomen. Fuck, she looked so goddamn *mine*.

The song ended and she bent into an overexaggerated curtsy. I clapped for her performance like I was a fan at one of my shows. "Wow, quite a hidden talent." I winked, the alcohol swirling round my body removing all inhibitions, letting me flirt with careless abandon.

"Shut up! I know I won't be selling out arenas anytime soon." She took a sip of her beer. "Go on, show me how it's done!" She held out the mic to me.

"No, no, I've got to protect the instrument." I tapped my throat, and she rolled her eyes. As true as that was, I'd never been much of a front man. I much preferred the comfort of being in the background, singing the odd backing vocal or two and chatting with the crowd but having none of the pressure to lead the stage and bring the star power. That was the best thing about being a band, not having to be up there alone with a single spotlight focussed on just me.

"Oh, come on." She pleaded. "For me?" She fluttered her long eyelashes and all I could imagine was her begging on her knees for me. In an attempt to limit my filthy thoughts I obliged, taking the mic.

"We're doing a duet though." I insisted as she began to search for the perfect number for us to perform to a crowd of zero. "I'm in a band not a soloist remember?" I chuckled, settling on a song I guaranteed we would both know well.

By the time we tumbled out of the bar, the sun had gone down and the chilly night air hit us. Amelia crossed her arms trying to preserve some heat.

"That was SO much fun! I've never done anything like that before. I've always been too self-conscious, but it felt good doing it with you." She laughed, high on adrenaline and alcohol.

"I'm proud of you, Sunflower." I nudged her, I knew she wouldn't take the praise, but I had to be honest. The hours had flown by as we sang countless songs, getting closer with every verse and I'd near on forgotten a world outside of that booth existed.

There were so many times I wished I could have pulled her in and made certain she knew how special she was. But despite my drunken haze I knew the reality of our situation and I couldn't risk our friendship.

15

AMELIA

I stumbled on uneven ground and grabbed for Theo's hand before I came face to face with the cobbles below.

"Careful, Sunflower," he chuckled, "someone's tipsy." I let go of his hand as quickly as I'd clasped it, the spark of his touch taking me by surprise.

"Shut up." I laughed, slightly breathless from tripping. Without thinking I linked my arm with his for stability, he looked down at me, clearly taken aback by the physical contact. Unlike most people, Theo's proximity never bothered me but it wasn't normal for me to initiate it. "Where to next?"

"You want more? Cor, haven't you had enough treats?" He winked, "It's like it's your birthday or something." I slapped his shoulder.

"Just not ready to end the night yet." I confessed, Theo smiled in agreement and I felt as if he was holding back saying something.

"Let's go sit on that wall." He pointed towards
the sea where wide concrete slabs edged the street,
overlooking the water. It was a cold night but the air was
fresh and truth be told it was helping to organise the
thoughts in my drunken mind.

We settled onto the makeshift seating area,
hanging our legs over the edge, looking out over the
moonlit water and listened to the waves lapping at the
shore.

"Wait here a second." Theo said before darting
off towards the lit buildings as if a lightbulb went off in
his head moments before.

I looked up at the stars, exhaling heavily as I
thought over the events of the day. Other than the
disappointment this morning, the rest of my birthday had
been unexpectedly perfect.

I hated to admit it but a large part of me knew for
certain that if my original plans had followed suit, then I
wouldn't be ending my day in quite as positive a mood.

A few minutes of peaceful contemplation passed
before I heard the patter of footsteps approaching me. I
turned to see Theo with a large carrier bag on his arm
and a bottle of wine in his hand. He held the drink up
and nodded towards me, I couldn't help the butterflies
swarming in my stomach as he walked closer.

"Okay so not the most gourmet of meals," he
announced, taking a seat beside me, "but figured you'd be
hungry and you can't go wrong with chips and dip,
right?" He pulled out a pot of aioli and a bag of tortilla

chips. "And then to wash it down, a bottle of the corner shop's finest white!"

"Aww, Theo, that sounds perfect!" I opened the packet of crisps, and Theo unscrewed the wine. "Glasses?"

"I warned you it wasn't gourmet." He smirked before taking a swig straight from the bottle. My eyes followed the movement, I watched his Adam's apple bob as he swallowed the drink, heat prickling between my legs. The combination of alcohol and not having sex for a while was definitely to blame for the unforeseen arousal.

"Give it here then." I grabbed the bottle from him and took a sip of my own to clear my inebriated mind. I tried not to notice Theo gazing at me the same way I had him moments before.

I turned back to look at Theo as he cleared his throat, catching my attention. He was holding a small satin box in his hands.

"Are you proposing to me, Theo?" I joked, flicking my eyes to the object.

"You should be so lucky, cutie," he winked passing me the gift. "It's not a birthday without a present."

I took it off him and slowly opened the lid to reveal a stunning pair of amber drop earrings, in a gold setting.

"I saw them in Paris and thought they were perfect for you. I hope you them like them. If you don't, feel free to sell them," he chuckled sheepishly, rubbing his neck with his hand.

"I love them, Theo. Honestly." His eyes lit up, "this is too much. You've done too much."

"Not at all, you deserve the world." He smiled warmly before diverting his gaze out to the waves ahead. I stared down at the jewels glinting from the light of the streetlamps, astonished at the gesture. I had never received anything that thoughtful before. Shutting the box, I was lost for words.

"Thank you, Theo." I replied simply. He nodded, his attention still on the horizon. I placed the object in my pocket and joined him in listening to the sound of the water crashing against the rocks below us. Theo leant back on his palms and closed his eyes.

"It's so nice to get out of the hotel rooms and experience the city a bit. Best part of touring in my opinion. Well except from the shows," he laughed awkwardly as if concerned that he had scorned his audience.

"Don't worry, Theo, this is off the record. I won't quote you on the blog, your fans won't think they're second best to a Portuguese coastline." I giggled. I looked at him and stared a little too long, really noticing for the first time his strong jawline decorated with dark stubble, the sharp angle of his nose and his unruly locks, displaced by the sea air. In the delicate glow of the moonlight, he was undeniably beautiful.

His full lips stretched into a cocky smirk. "Take a picture, Sunflower. It'll last longer." He laughed with his eyes still closed. Heat rushed to my cheeks, how did he know I was gawking? Presumably he could feel the intensity of the way I was observing him.

"As you wish." I took out my phone and snapped a quick picture.

"One for the blog?" He smirked, his eyelids fluttering open.

"Nah, this one's for me." I giggled drunkenly, slipping my phone back into my jean pocket.

Any further sarcastic remark I could have made died on my tongue as he shot me a wink. I refocused on the scene in front of me, whatever was happening between us was unexplainable and I knew allowing myself to enjoy the feeling was dangerous but I couldn't convince myself to care.

Theo sat up and rifled through the bag to his side. "Close your eyes and hold out your hands." I did as he requested, at this point I would have done damn near anything he asked.

I heard a clink of metal followed by a flick which I recognised as the sound of a lighter igniting. Cold foil touched my palm, as the feeling of two warm hands cupped the underside of mine. "Open your eyes, Sunflower."

As the scene came back into view, I caught my breath at the sight of the pastel de nata balanced on my skin with a candle in the top, burning with an orange glow. "Seeing as we didn't get to do this earlier, happy birthday, Amelia." Theo smiled through the orange light, the flicker of the flame reflecting in his hazel eyes. The lighter not only ignited the candle but also the fire in my stomach. "Make a wish." Theo whispered. The way he was looking at me was downright sinful.

There was only one thing I could imagine in that moment, and as wrong as it was to be wishing for it, I leant forward slowly and blew out the candle, not breaking eye contact. Theo rolled his lips, his eyes drinking me in. He dropped his hands away from mine and I placed the tart onto the concrete.

"So, is Lisbon your favourite city yet?" I asked, breaking the silence and *trying* to break whatever spell I was under. The wind whipped around us, displacing my curls.

"Hmm, it's definitely up there." Theo reached towards me, tucking my hair behind my ear, my breath hitched at the movement.

"What was your favourite part?" I asked shakily, his hand resting on my jawline.

"The company." He stated simply, guiding my face towards his. I let myself go, desperate to feel his lips against mine. His breath ghosted across my mouth, "Theo." I whispered unsure if I was shutting him down or welcoming him.

At the sound of his name coated with uncertainty, he broke the contact. "Sorry, Sunflower." He ran a hand through his hair and turned his attention to the choppy waves. Breathless, I took a moment to attempt to collect my thoughts, the air around me was frigid without his touch. Although I didn't know if I was relieved or disappointed, one thing was for certain, I didn't want him to feel bad for the action. I shuffled towards him and leant my head on his shoulder. "Don't be. It's been the best birthday ever."

Instinctively, he laid his head on top of mine, just like that night in the hotel room in Madrid, it was fast becoming our 'thing'. "I'm glad, as I said, you deserve it." He responded. I recognised an edge in his voice that was different to the happy-go-lucky tone he usually spoke with, as if he was battling his own internal mental activity. "It's getting cold out, let's get you back to the hotel."

In near silence, we hailed a cab and returned to our accommodation. As with all the previous hotels, our rooms were only a few doors apart. We reached mine, lingering for a moment at the entrance to the room. A metre or so of space between us. "Goodnight, Sunflower."

"Goodnight, Theo." I replied. He rubbed his neck, opened his mouth to speak before smiling and wandering down the remainder of the hall to his own room. I didn't move until he had disappeared completely from view.

Entering my suite, I dropped my jacket onto the bed and took a seat on the chair by the dressing table. Confused feelings swirled around my head as I stared at my reflection in the mirror. I didn't know what I wanted or what I needed but the six-foot guitarist, four doors down, was burning a hole in my mind. Feeling as if the night ended with words unsaid, I decided I had to speak to him. Now.

I opened the large wooden door to my suite and froze.

"Theo," I said, barely audible. He looked as conflicted and surprised as I felt. Before I had fully acknowledged his presence, he took my face in both of his hands and crashed his mouth to mine. The relief of his lips on my own was mesmerising. I couldn't place the tension before but now the elastic band had snapped it was clear we had been holding ourselves back all day. Subconsciously, I fisted the material of his t-shirt, feeling the outline of his muscled chest under my hand. As I began to move my mouth in time with his, he ended the kiss abruptly.

"I'm sorry but I just had to do that. Just once." He stated, looking into my eyes, releasing his grip. For the first time in the several years I'd known him I couldn't read his expression. Before I had the chance to respond, he turned on his heels, leaving me dumbfounded in the doorway.

Returning to my bed, I lay against the soft pillows, trying to make sense of the day. A wave of guilt coursed through my veins. It was so unlike me to act this way and risk the trust of Josh but I had also never felt the way in which I felt tonight and that only made matters worse.

My phone beeped causing me to jump. I told my subconscious that I didn't want it to be *him*. Fishing the device out of my pocket. I breathed a half-sigh of relief at the message from Josh, he was the person I should want to contact me at this hour.

I opened the photo that accompanied the text. A shiver ran through me as I gazed at my boyfriend's naked torso with the corner of a blanket carefully strewn across his groin. I bit my lip feeling the arousal churn in my core. This was what I needed. Finally, the confusion cleared, I had been missing my boyfriend and mistook kindness from a friend today as something more. God, I was a mess. I needed to do something about this.

I took off my trousers and took one last look at the image as I slipped my hand under the hem of my underwear. I groaned as I felt the slickness between my thighs, telling myself the unexpected kiss had nothing to do with it. Squeezing my eyes shut, I pictured Josh above me and what he would be doing to me if he was here right now. I began to circle my clit with my fingers. My other hand trailed up my torso towards my hardened nipple.

As I lifted my t-shirt the familiar spicy smell of Theo's cologne swirled into my consciousness, from the Paper Sunsets tee I was still wearing. The image shifted: straight blonde hair morphed into thick dark curls; blue eyes turned muddy-green; lean shoulders became broader and more muscular. I panted as Theo's face became crystal clear in my imagination taking pride of place within this illicit fantasy. My pace quickened as flashbacks of today played on a loop. His cocky smirk as he watched me dance in the karaoke booth; the feel of his breath as it tickled over my lips by the sea and the dominance of the

kiss just minutes ago that knocked me off guard. I
clenched my thighs together and pinched my nipple as I
worked myself further to ecstasy. It would have been so
easy to march to his room and replace my hand with his
mouth. The forbidden thought tipped me over the edge
and I threw my head back as I shuddered through my
climax.

As I came down from my high, my stomach
lurched with guilt.

Oh fuck!

16

THEO

Well, the events of Amelia's birthday were unexpected to say the least and I had most definitely crossed several moral lines.

I didn't care for Josh; in fact I despised the man, but I thought myself better than to pursue a taken woman so obtusely. It wasn't fair to put her in that position. Even if it was obvious she wasn't happy in her relationship, until she worked out for herself that she deserved better, I needed to dial it back and not impose my own opinions on her. But her brazen flirting and the way she was looking at me that night was intoxicating. I may have been acting on impulse, but I wasn't reading things that weren't there. As much as she wasn't ready to admit it to herself there was a part of her that wanted me.

It had been nearly a week since the stolen kiss and we had played two sold out shows and were now back on the road to Amsterdam. Thankfully mine and the curly-haired vixen's relationship had been unaffected by the complications. However, whilst we were all cooped up on the tour bus for hours, I was trying to keep some distance to avoid getting myself into trouble.

"Fuck sake mate, you keep getting us killed!" Callum complained, gesturing to the screen. "Get your head in the game."

"Sorry man, I wasn't concentrating," I confessed, shaking my head to rid any confusing trails of thought and recentre on the first-person shooter game that we were playing together.

"Yeah, no shit!" Sean laughed, unbothered as he and Finn won yet another round due to my inability to focus.

"Millie, could you take his spot please? This is embarrassing!" Callum called through to Amelia who was working on the table at the other end of the bus.

"Sorry, Callum, I'm busy. You'll have to put up with Shit Shot in there." Despite the insult, the giggle in her voice warmed my heart.

"Ugh, for fuck's sake." Cal groaned, throwing his hands up in the air.

"Tell ya what, Theo, can you come here for a sec?" She called, ushering me towards her.

"Yeah, good idea, I'd rather be completely solo than have the deadweight." I jabbed Callum in the shoulder for his insult as I stood up.

"How can I be of service?" I asked, plonking myself in the seat opposite her.

She spun her laptop to face me, "can you proofread this before I post it?"

"Sure, Sunflower." I began to read the article taking in every word but knowing that obviously I wasn't going to critique her work. There was a reason she was in charge of our socials and not me.

"I'm not sure on this bi-" She reached over, to point to a particular paragraph. As she did, her forearm knocked into her full glass of iced coffee, spilling the contents all over the table and onto me. Quickly I picked up the laptop but couldn't save my white shirt in time.

"Fuck, I'm so so sorry!" She spluttered, reaching across to pick up the vessel before taking the MacBook off me and placing it on the chair beside her.

She frantically grabbed a tea towel from the counter behind and simultaneously dried the table as well as dabbing at my top.

"Mils, it's fine, I think it might take a spin cycle or two to clean this out rather than a light pat." I laughed, pointing at the large brown stain that had quickly formed.

"Shit." She concluded, taking her hand off me. "I guess this is the last time you're going to help me with anything." She joked, clearly still embarrassed.

"Don't be silly," I stood up and pulled the shirt over my head. "Give me that," I took the cloth from her hand and dried the excess liquid off my abs. I caught a look at her face, which was fixed on my bare skin. A twitch shot to my cock as she dragged an appreciative gaze along my frame, her mouth popped open half an inch.

No, no, no. We are not going there. I mentally scolded myself for the explicit thoughts entering my subconscious. "It was great by the way." I told her, beginning to walk to my bag, hanging up by my bunk, to find another shirt.

"What was?" She tore her eyes away from my naked skin, "your coffee shower?" A sheepish laugh slipped past her lips.

I turned back to her. "No, the post. No notes." I said, nodding towards her laptop. I retrieved a replacement top and rejoined the boys in the lounge area. Callum threw me a concerned look as I sat cross legged beside him again. "Don't worry, I'm not in the mood to game now. I'm just gonna watch." The boys breathed a sigh of relief and continued with their battle.

Internally I cursed myself for how complicated I had made things in Lisbon. I didn't regret any of my actions but I would *not* be doing it again. That kiss was a line drawn. She had a boyfriend; we were just friends and it was about time that I moved on.

17

AMELIA

Knock knock!

The familiar sound of Theo rapping on my door caught my attention away from the photos I was editing for the blog.

Regardless of what had occurred at the end of my birthday, I was glad that Theo was acting normal around me. Although he initiated the kiss, I wasn't totally innocent. There was a part of me that enjoyed indulging in the compliments and affection that Theo gave me that day. I wasn't used to being made the centre of attention and definitely didn't do anything to reduce it - even when I knew it was too much. I swore to myself it was a one off and that it was meaningless. Without having to have the awkward conversation, it thankfully appeared that Theo was on the same page, it was as if it had never happened!

With anticipation of what plan Theo had up his sleeve today, I strolled leisurely to let him in. Every city on the tour so far, we had killed time prior to the shows and days off, mooching around the local towns, finding delicious places to eat and interesting shops. It had become a ritual that I couldn't wait for each time we crossed the border into new unexplored territory.

I opened the door to find an unexpected visitor.

"Hey, Aims." Josh greeted. I stood frozen in the entranceway, unable to speak. A mix of emotions flooded through me. Surprise swirled with guilt from the events of Lisbon and *further* guilt that I didn't feel nearly happy enough seeing him standing there.

"What are you doing here?" I tried not to sound accusatory. He raised a confused eyebrow, "I mean, it's great to see you but why are you *here?* In Amsterdam?"

"I wanted to surprise my girlfriend, is that a crime?" He chuckled, with a slight edge to his voice. "Gonna give me a kiss then?"

I regained control over my body and wrapped my arms around his neck, placing a chaste kiss to his lips. There was no spark of electricity, no butterflies fluttering in my stomach and no desire for more. Something had changed.

I pulled back abruptly. "I missed you." I whispered half-heartedly, trying to distract him from my lack of enthusiasm.

"You too." He concluded, slipping out of my arms and stepping past me into my room. "So, this is the groupie lifestyle then, is it?" He said, sounding unimpressed by my accommodation which was surprising considering it was a five-star suite in one of the best hotels in the city, but I guess Josh set impossible standards for hotels too, not just his girlfriend.

"I'm not a groupie." I stated, feeling uncharacteristically irritated by his thinly veiled dig. It would appear that the time apart had only made me less tolerant of his shitty attitude.

I guess in this case, absence didn't make the heart grow fonder.

He sat on the edge of my bed, leaning back on his palms, with a seductive look in his eyes. As he opened his mouth to speak, I cut him off. "I'm hungry, shall we go and get something to eat?" It sounded awful but I wanted to get out of this room and away from the prospect of having sex. I was not in the mood or the right frame of mind to give myself to him right now.

"Sure, is there a Maccy's local?" He asked. Trust Josh to travel to another country and crave a Big Mac.

"We're in Amsterdam Josh; we can have a McDonalds in London." I rolled my eyes, crossing my arms.

"What do you want instead, a spliff? Hash cake?" He chuckled to himself. I stared blankly back at him.

"No Josh, let's just go and have a look around some cafes." I suggested, heading towards the exit. I heard him huff as he hauled himself off my bed and followed close behind.

After meandering down several streets, we 'compromised' and went to McDonalds. Once we had ordered our food, I managed to convince him to at least sit by the canal to enjoy some of the sights.

"What did you do for your birthday then?" Josh asked, chomping down on a handful of fries. It had been a week since then but unsurprisingly, this was the first time he had asked about the day, which he had let me down.

"We went out in the city and did lots of various activities! Wine tasting, karaoke." My mind replayed the day and I actively avoided telling him who I had been with or the moments by the sea. It wasn't lost on me, the juxtaposition between the thoughtful moments I shared with Theo on the seawall and the careless moment I was now experiencing with Josh.

"We?" He queried; it felt like a loaded question disguised as interest.

"Well yeah, I wasn't going to spend it alone. I was with the band." I shrugged; the lie slipped out too easily but my stomach twisted with guilt. There was no reason not to tell him the truth but something was holding me back.

"Riiiight," he elongated the word as if he was assessing my answer, "do you have any photos of your special day out?" Josh requested, jealousy coating his words.

I opened my phone and began to swipe through the images from the fun-filled day that Theo had curated. There were pictures of me with various glasses of wine, dancing in the karaoke booth and walking down the cobbled streets of Portugal, smiling into the lens. As I reached the final few, one appeared onscreen of Theo relaxing on the seawall, eyes closed with the moonlight reflecting across his face. "That's the last one." I concluded, quickly flicking to a random screenshot that was saved in my gallery, to get it off my screen.

"Were the other three camera shy?" Josh queried with no emotion.

"You know Theo, he loves to hog the camera. The others didn't stand a chance."

Josh nodded slowly, taking in my words. The blood in my veins turned to ice as the surprise kiss that occurred later that same evening sprang to the forefront of my mind. I hated lying to him and what I had allowed to happen. I was not a cheater, that title sat better with Josh, but here I was, sitting on a bench in Amsterdam, deceiving him right to his face.

"I'm getting cold, can we go back now?" I requested, praying that the change in scenery would alter the topic of conversation.

He shrugged in agreement and we walked in silence back to the hotel.

We stepped out of the elevator onto my level and as if God was laughing at me, who should be standing in the hallway waiting for the very same lift we were occupying? Theo Hart.

He looked up from his phone.

"Oh, hello Joshua, what a lovely surprise!" Theo greeted with a shit-eating grin, once he'd registered who was in front of him.

"Likewise." Josh responded blankly, as we stepped out of the box. My heart was pounding in my chest. I was trying to communicate telepathically with Theo to not be a prick and wind him up further.

"We missed you in Lisbon, we had a great day. Didn't we, Sunflower?" He smirked and I internally cringed at the use of my nickname in front of my boyfriend.

"Mmhmm." I hummed non-committedly. Josh didn't respond. I could feel him vibrating with frustration to my side and braced myself for the next interaction. Unsure whether he was about to burst into explosive accusations or punch the cocky smile off Theo's face. Theo, on the other hand, seemed completely unbothered. If anything, he almost appeared to be enjoying watching Josh squirm.

"Anyway, I won't hold you lovebirds up any longer," I breathed a sigh of relief as he finally cottoned on to the warning look I was shooting his way. "I'll catch you at the show tonight." He saluted and shuffled past us into the lift.

We continued towards my room and I felt heat prickle at the back of my spine from Josh's glare as he sauntered behind me. I didn't rise to his attitude, I knew how he felt about Theo at the best of times, but I wouldn't have imagined the first time that they saw each other on tour would be so frosty.

I gestured for Josh to enter my hotel room before closing the door behind us. As soon as we were alone, he finally spoke.

"Well, that was nice." Josh spat through a forced smile. "Always *such* a pleasure to see Theo, isn't it?"

I daren't respond knowing whatever I said right now would be misconstrued or misinterpreted. "Tea?" He shook his head but I began to boil the small kettle on top of the desk nevertheless, opting to stay busy. "So anywhere or anything you want to do now?" I asked, in an attempt to move the conversation away from the cocksure guitarist.

"Do you wear all the band member's tops then? Or just the ones you go on dates with?" He ignored me, asking the question that must have been burning in his mind. Heat rushed to my face at the accusation and the realisation that Theo was wearing the same fucking Paper Sunsets t-shirt, that I had just shown Josh I was wearing in Lisbon. I hadn't even noticed!

I panicked for a response, finding it hard to defend myself. Although, I'm sure at that moment Josh cemented his belief that I had slept with Theo and in that sense, I was innocent, but we were definitely not free from sin.

Just as my guilty conscience was about to take over, years of his infidelity rushed to the forefront of my mind. All I had done was spend my birthday with a friend and I wasn't going to let myself be condemned for it.

"I'm not going to dignify that with an answer, Josh. We need to get ready for the show."

18

THEO

"Thank you and goodnight, Amsterdam!" Sean called out to the electric crowd. This had easily been one of the best shows so far of the tour. The lyrics had been sung louder than ever before and the adrenaline I had felt had been stronger. Although I was sure that was thanks to a certain couple in front of the barricade.

My attention was caught multiple times throughout as Josh pulled Amelia to him or wrapped his arm around her waist, preventing her from moving along the edge of the stage as freely as she usually did. I had no right to feel jealous but I couldn't stop the irritation bubbling in my stomach. Yet, each time she shrugged him off to resume snapping pictures of me or the other boys, that annoyance was quickly extinguished and replaced with satisfaction.

In fact, by the second half, I was enjoying winding him up by flirting shamelessly with the camera and the woman behind the lens. It only egged me on further when she had nearly ditched him all together, clearly preferring my cocky smirks to Josh's (admittedly warranted) scowls.

As the lights dimmed, we ran off stage and regrouped in the green room. "What's the plan then, lads?" Callum asked, rubbing his hands together which were calloused from his drumsticks.

"Red light district?" Sean chuckled, wiggling his eyebrows suggestively. I rolled my eyes, giving him a playful shove.

"Count me out of that one." Finn laughed.

"And me." Amelia added, appearing at my side.

"I know a place." Josh's voice cut through like nails on a chalkboard. We turned to look at him, the boys clearly confused as to who the fuck he was.

"We're all ears, Joshua." I encouraged sarcastically, catching Amelia's eye, "this is Mils' boyfriend by the way." I introduced him to the group, only to be met with half smiles and raised eyebrows as they put two and two together – that he was the infamous philanderer who's partner I was head over heels for. I hoped that for once they would decide to leave the usual jokes about my infatuation with Amelia unspoken. As Josh shook their hands, Amelia mouthed 'be nice' to me out of view of the rest of the group. 'Okay, okay,' I telepathically said back, raising my eyebrows.

"It's called Dam Good Bar." Josh declared.

"Well, if the name's anything to go by, it sounds perfect, mate." I slapped him on the back slightly harder than necessary, "lead the way!" I winked at Amelia without Josh seeing, conveying the message that I could play nice if I wanted to. She bit her lip, holding back a giggle.

We began to follow Josh out of the venue and onto the streets of Amsterdam. Any fans that had been lingering to see us had now dissipated and we made our way towards my new best mate's venue of choice. Although Josh wouldn't usually be involved in my ideal post-show ritual, there was a part of me that got a sick thrill from toying with him in front of Amelia. I knew each individual comment was toeing the line between aggravating and entertaining her.

To give Josh some credit, the bar was heaving when we arrived. The six of us made our way through the crowd out the front and through to the bar.

"Joshy boy!" A man with a cockney accent shouted over to him.

"Timsta!" Josh called back as the pair hugged in a greeting.

"You were longer than expected." *Timsta* said.

"Yeah, I got caught up at that gig didn't I, but I'm here now, that's all that matters. Time to get the bevvies in!" Josh transformed into 'Ultimate Lad' before my eyes and I tried not to gag. Every time I had the displeasure of seeing this man, I was left baffled at how Amelia put up with him.

"Wahey, the other lads are just over there. Let's get this party started!" The man, who I assumed was actually called Tim, gestured to the back of the bar, raising his hands up and down like a fucking loser. "See you over there." He said, heading back towards his table.

"Josh, what are your friends doing here?" Amelia's shaky voice pricked my ears up over the blaring music. I had been so focused on Josh and his 'ultimate banter' that it hadn't occurred to me who how out of the norm this meeting was or how it might have made her feel.

"Well Tim had planned a birthday trip here this weekend and it lined up with you - how perfect!" He declared looking rather pleased with himself, "you know, two birds and all that." Funny how he could make the effort for his bro's birthday and not his girlfriend of six years...

"So, you didn't come to see *me* then?" She probed.

"I'm here aren't I, Aims? I *have* seen you." He shrugged. I tried my best not to eavesdrop but the pain on her face and heartbreak in her voice kept dragging my attention back to the squabbling pair.

"Yeah, but just as a gap in your friend's itinerary." She looked so hurt as she realised, she hadn't been his priority. Again.

"Fucking hell, you always ask me to be spontaneous and surprise you, then I fucking do and you're not happy! Damned if I do, damned if I fucking don't." He shouted, throwing his hands up in the air. I wanted nothing more than to punch the attitude out of him. Instead, I clenched my jaw, knowing this wasn't my fight.

I felt someone nudge my arm, "we're gonna go," Finn started, pointing towards the smoking area. "Give these two a minute." He whispered.

I knew listening in wasn't the right thing to do but something was preventing me from walking away. "I'll get our drinks, meet you in a minute," I replied, turning towards the bar, still within earshot of the pair arguing.

When I glanced back to the scene; Amelia was crying, her voice less audible through sobs, my body tensed as I resisted the urge to pull her into my arms. "Can you honestly not understand why I'm upset? I've not seen you in weeks and when I do, you've not prioritised me."

I watched Josh shrug from the corner of my eye. "Let's be real, Aims, you've hardly been fucking lonely without me, have ya?" Josh dug in the knife and twisted it. I swallowed a lump that was in my throat. I understood Josh's implication, that she had been unfaithful whilst on the road. Presumably with *me*, no doubt.

She stood speechless, tears rolling down her cheeks as she registered his words.

"I'm done Josh. I can't do this anymore." She turned on her heels. Instinctively, I reached out to grab her shoulder as she passed me.

"Do you want me to come with you?" I offered, looking deep into her heartbroken eyes.

"No," she sniffled, "I want to be alone." She moved out of my grip and pushed through the throngs of revellers, towards the exit. It pained me to see her go but just as I was about to follow her, Josh piped up.

"Trust you to go scurrying off after her to wipe away her tears. I bet this is what you've been praying for. For me to fuck up." Josh's anger redirected to me now that we were alone.

"Let's be real if I did want that, I wouldn't have to pray hard Josh, you're always fucking up." I spat, my voice coated in venom. Just in the past couple of months alone, I would have run out of fingers to count on if I recalled all the times Josh had upset Amelia.

"Well congratulations Theo, you got what you wanted. She's all yours now." He waved a dismissive hand towards me, as if she was an object that could be passed around with no say in the matter.

"What are you on about?" Rage bubbled below the surface as I balled my fists at my side.

"Don't treat me like an idiot. I heard the details of your little *date* in Lisbon and I saw the way you gawked at her on stage, and what's this Sunflower bullshit?" I rolled my eyes as he continued to rant, squaring up to me, all five foot six of him. "Not to mention, all your fucking songs are about her. A blind man could see you've wanted her from the start."

No matter how much I wanted to deck him, I knew he wasn't worth it. I took a deep breath to release the anger coursing through every vein in my body and walked away.

"Whatever, mate."

19

AMELIA

I stormed down the busy road, lined with bars and revellers all having a much better evening than me.

I should have known that Josh wouldn't have gone out of his way to visit me without it being of some other benefit to him also. My stupid blind optimism had gotten the better of me yet again.

As I hurried down the street, the familiar scars on my heart from our previous breakups burst open like fresh wounds. The tears ran down my face continuously and I heaved for breath as our relationship fell to pieces for what felt like the hundredth time. I should be used to this by now, it shouldn't hurt this much but I'd given so many years of my life to him only for it to fail once more.

Over the rushing in my ears, the sound of footsteps coming closer caught my attention.

"What part of I'm done don't you understand? I don't want to speak to you right now, Josh." I spat out, not bothering to turn. I had nothing left to say to him tonight.

"It's me." Theo's voice took me by surprise as he replied, I froze and whipped around to face him.

"I said I wanted to be alone." I protested, crossing my arms over my body.

Theo caught up to where I was standing and half-smiled. "I know you did but I know that's not true." He reached out towards me and I backed away. Theo flinched at my reaction before dropping his hand awkwardly.

"What makes you so sure? You seem to think you know me so well. Always coming in to save the day like a knight in shining armour." My voice came out harsher than I was expecting but I was running on anger and didn't want the pity party. A flicker of pain crossed Theo's features as my words sunk in.

"I care about you." He sighed, avoiding eye contact momentarily.

I let out a bitter laugh. "Too much, Theo, I'm not your fucking girlfriend."

He tensed his jaw. "I'm well aware of that, Amelia." I could see my words were hurting him but I couldn't stop my tirade, it was like word vomit.

I took a step towards him, "so why did you kiss me?" The question fell from my lips before I had a chance to register it. Theo looked shocked, neither of us had mentioned the kiss since it happened, both silently agreeing to sweep it under the rug. His eyes hardened once again before he dug for his own information.

"Why were you leaving your room? Where were you going that night?" He deflected, defiantly avoiding my interrogation.

I couldn't answer, I knew exactly where I was headed but I was yet to figure out why. The pull of Theo's room had been too strong to resist. I stood frozen, my mouth opening and shutting, resembling a fish, as I tried to think of a coherent response.

The silence stretched out between us. "I could make a pretty good guess." Theo scoffed, staring me down.

"Fuck off, Theo." I cursed, "Why can't you just be my friend?" A sob escaped my lips. I turned away from him and marched on towards the solitude of the hotel. I couldn't discuss the topic that we had both actively avoided. Not tonight, not on top of all the other shit.

As the space between where Theo and I had just stood grew further, I couldn't bear to turn back to see if he remained in the spot, where I had spoken to him so badly. I didn't want to see the look on his face, that I caused, by dismissing him. Or worse, to see that he wasn't standing there at all. That he had done as I demanded and left, confirming that I had succeeded in pushing away the one person who truly seemed to care for me.

20

THEO

I watched for a few seconds as she hastily walked away. After debating following her again, I decided it was best to do as she asked and let her go. The last thing I wanted was to disrespect her wishes, she knew what she needed right now. It killed me to turn around. My heart was screaming at me to wrap her in my arms and take the pain away but I forced my legs to move in the opposite direction.

Amelia? I thought as I turned the corner of the street in my car. It was a crisp October evening accompanied by a rainstorm. No one should be meandering down the road in this weather or at this time!

I slowed down beside her and wound down the window. "Hey, Mils, get in the car!" I called out. She barely acknowledged me. "Amelia!" I shouted louder and beeped my horn. She jolted as I broke her out of a thought.

She paused for a second, as if building up to decline my offer. I pointed to the dark grey sky, rain pouring endlessly over her. Her expression softened and she nodded before crossing the road to get in the passenger seat.

Only after she was in the vehicle did I realise the rain had been disguising her tears.

"Hey, what's up?" I asked, pulling up the handbrake and placing a comforting hand on her shoulder. She sniffled, wiping under her eyes.

"It's nothing, I'm fine." She lied.

"It's clearly not, you're walking in the rain at 11pm as if you're in a sad music video." Her lips pulled up into a half smile that looked more like a grimace. I was certain now wasn't the time for jokes but for all the times I had crossed paths with Amelia, our relationship had never ventured into 'agony aunt' territory, so I didn't know the best way to play this.

Although she'd never told me herself, I knew through Lilah and her friends that Amelia's boyfriend treated her pretty terribly. I didn't want to wrongly assume but if I was to place bets…

"You're clearly busy, Theo; you don't want to listen to my sob story." She stared out of the window, the rumble of the engine filling the silences.

"Try me."

"My boyfriend stood me up."

"What? Your long-term boyfriend?" I replied to the back of her head. How can someone be stood up by the person they're in a serious relationship with?

"Yeah, I didn't even think that was possible, thought that was reserved to first dates only y'know?" She laughed sadly *mirroring my internal thoughts, finally looking at me. Her brown eyes, round and full of tears. I resisted the urge to wipe them away.*

"Prick." I said bitterly.

"I gave up waiting for him and tried to hail a cab to no avail. Hence the drowned rat appearance." She continued, glazing over the insult.

"Well, I'm glad I bumped into you, it's freezing out tonight."

"Ha, my knight in shining armour."

"If you need me to be." I stared at her a little too long. Even with puffy red eyes from crying and soaked to the core by rain, she was beautiful.

A car beeped from behind my stationary vehicle that was blocking the road. In sync, we both looked through the back window. A man behind the steering wheel was throwing his hands up in the air – patience of a gnat that one!

"You can drive, Theo, I'm fine, really." She breathed, mere inches from my face. My eyes flicked to her lips momentarily.

"Not until I'm sure you're okay. I'll sit here all night if I must." I sat back in my seat and turned the engine off.

The car behind beeped more furiously. I just folded my arms in defiance.

"Theo!" Amelia giggled, turning her attention to me and then back to the angry driver. "I'm better I promise." She flashed me the widest, cheesiest grin. I turned the engine back on and released the handbrake.

Dawdling back to the bar reminiscing over the first time Amelia confided in me, I prayed I wouldn't bump into the cunt that caused her heartbreak.

After recent events, I wasn't feeling too interested in socialising but fuck, I needed a drink.

Pushing through the front door of the venue, I spotted the band immediately, chatting away to a group of girls that I didn't recognise.

"Ah, Theo, you're back," Finn greeted, handing me a pint of beer. It was as if he had read my mind, "where's Mils? I got her usual."

"She's gone mate." The knife twisted in my gut as I said it out loud. "She didn't want me to follow."

"That's shit, she deserves better than that prick." I raised my eyebrows in agreement as I took a sip of my drink. "Speaking of, they've left by the way." I assumed 'they' was Josh and his ragtag bunch of lad clones. Thank fuck for that.

"Who are our new friends?" I nodded towards the four strangers who were now integrated with my bandmates.

"Not a fucking clue mate, Sean called them over." He laughed. It wasn't out of the ordinary for the boys to invite people to join us, especially given how much Callum and Sean loved the ladies, in particular. Finn was different, although he was never short of female attention, he never actively went looking for it.

"You must be, Theo?" A stunning brunette asked, catching my attention. I painted a half-arsed smile on my face. Finn held his drink up to me as a goodbye, disappearing into the crowd whilst flicking through his phone.

"Who's asking?" I joked, my usual charm returning. Her hourglass frame slid into the space Finn had just occupied and she began to suck on the straw of her drink.

"Amy, but you can call me Aims." Perfect, of course that's her fucking name, as if I needed Amelia on my mind any more than she already was. I looked past her and made eye contact with Callum who had his arm wrapped around a blonde woman. He nodded towards me, smiling like the cat who got the cream.

I turned at the feeling of a tap on my shoulder. Finn had returned and was leaning into my ear, "I spoke to her by the way. She's back at the hotel."

"Oh, appreciate it man." I thanked. I hadn't realised how wound up I had been following my argument with Amelia. Now that I knew she was safe, I felt like I could finally relax somewhat and try to forget about her for a night.

"I heard about your show," Amy drew my focus back to her. "I'd love to come and see it one night!" She blinked her green eyes up at me.

"Well, we've got another tomorrow. But it's sold out I'm afraid." I shot her a wink and watched her cheeks blush.

"Maybe I could get to know a member of the band?" She traced the rim of her glass with her finger and licked her lips seductively.

"Flirting for a backstage pass, huh?" A genuine smirk pulled at my lips.

She took a step closer, placing her hand on my chest. "Is it working?"

"Perhaps." I'd missed this. The ease of talking to a girl without complications or deep feelings. "So, tell me about yourself?"

The next couple of hours passed in a blur as Amy and I separated from the group. I hadn't been interested in meeting anyone but she was sweet, so I hadn't felt the need to immediately shut it down this evening.

As the bar closed, the rest of the band and their respective newfound partners decided they weren't ready to call it a night. However, after the drama with Josh and Amelia and the numerous pints I had sunk, my bed was calling.

"I'm getting pretty tired too," Amy agreed as I started to say goodbye.

"Where are you staying?" I asked, assuming she wasn't local from her strong Californian accent. She typed in the address of her accommodation, which was only round the corner from mine. "I'll walk you back."

We meandered through the streets of Amsterdam, continuing our easy conversation. She took my hand in hers and I didn't protest as we walked side by side until her hotel came into view.

"This is me," she gestured to the grand foyer of the building. "I'm glad I bumped into you."

"Likewise, darling." I smiled, tucking her dark hair behind her ear. She leant her face up towards mine and I captured her lips in a soft kiss. There was no reason for it but her lips tasted bitter as guilt swirled in my stomach.

"So..?" She whispered looking up at me, from under her lashes, a silent request to join her inside. Admittedly, I considered it. Some meaningless sex might have been just what I needed but I knew deep down, that wasn't what I wanted. Albeit that Amelia had very clearly rejected me this evening, my heart still yearned for her.

"So, come to the show tomorrow." I doused the flames of desire emanating from her. She pouted in protest. "I'll give you my number." I typed the digits into her phone which she had handed me.

"I look forward to it. See you tomorrow." She kissed me on the cheek before disappearing into the hotel.

21

AMELIA

I think I eventually fell asleep around 3am. Between the pain of the heartbreak, the guilt I felt for shouting at Theo and the overwhelming sense of loneliness, it had been impossible to switch my brain off.

On the surface, today had been on track to be much like any other show day. However, the first sign that something was off came around lunch, when my usual visitor failed to make an appearance. It wasn't until Theo didn't knock, that I realised just how much I missed it.

Theo and I had disagreed on plenty of things over the years that we had known each other; however, I had never raised my voice at him and the topic had never gotten that deep before.

I think what had hurt the most last night was that he hadn't been wrong. I had yet to admit it to myself so when he held up the mirror, I couldn't take it.

I *had* wanted to kiss him in Lisbon. I *was* heading to his room and as awful as it was to confess, I couldn't be certain that I wouldn't have crossed the line and betrayed Josh further had he invited himself inside.

As the hours passed by slowly, I distracted my confused and unsettled mind with work. I actively avoided the images I had snapped at last night's show, knowing it would hurt too much to see Theo happy and carefree prior to the fallout that later occurred. Opting instead, to write up the first draft of the recap of Amsterdam night one.

The afternoon drew to a close and my phone had remained silent. Arrogantly I had expected a message from Josh (or Theo) checking in - but was left forlorn when neither reached out.

I entered the foyer and found only Finn. "Just us or are we waiting for the others?"

"Just us I think, let's go!" Finn replied. It wasn't uncommon for the band to separate during the day and as long as everyone made it to the venue on time, there was never any issue in making our own ways to the gig.

"You sure you're feeling up to tonight?" Finn asked, once we settled into the taxi. I didn't know what Theo had told him but I appreciated the genuine care.

"Ah yeah, I'm fine. You know, this isn't exactly unusual in mine and Josh's relationship." I confessed, feeling a bit embarrassed for admitting that this was all just a part of our cycle. "Did you guys have a good rest of your night?"

"Yeah, it was pretty good. We made some buddies!" Finn chuckled slightly.

"I'm happy for you." I laughed, catching onto the meaning behind his words.

It wasn't long before we had reached the auditorium. When I walked into the green room, Sean and Callum were already inside, sipping a beer and chatting.

"There are the dirty stop outs!" I mocked.

"Don't hate us, cos you ain't us, Mils." Callum joked, "it was a good night! Although I saw more of Sean than I'd ever wished to see."

My eyes bulged. "Come again?"

"That's what she said!" Sean chimed in.

I chose to ignore his vulgar joke. "You were *together*?"

"Mils, these girls mate. They were unreal. There was no way I was going to say no, even if it meant seeing Sean balls deep." Callum gave me a look as if I should understand his reasoning.

"Hey, you saw a master at work. You probably learnt a thing or two." Sean winked.

"Okay, okay, leave me out of the boy talk please." I laughed, waving my hand dismissively, I did not need the image of Callum and Sean involved in a foursome floating around my subconscious.

"Where's Theo?" I asked nervously, noting his absence.

"Beats me, he left with a stunner. Maybe he's still shacked up with her." Sean bleated, my heart sank immediately. I tried not to picture the mystery woman and Theo spending the night together. I had no right to be feeling jealous but it didn't stop the green-eyed monster from rearing its ugly head.

"Hey guys, sorry I'm so late!" The sound of Theo's voice as he entered the doorway, made me whip my head around.

"Dirty stop out number three!" Finn chanted from across the room.

"Ah nah mate, I just lost track of time exploring the town." He responded, making a beeline for a can of his own. An unwarranted sense of relief ran through me at the confirmation he was alone. I stopped him halfway to the cooler, reaching out to touch his arm.

"Theo, can I talk to you quickly please?" I knew five minutes before the start of the show wasn't ideal timing but I couldn't go another couple of hours without clearing the air.

He nodded and we walked to a private corner.

"About last night, I'm really-"

"Don't sweat it, Sunflower." He smiled widely and all tension dissipated from my body. "There's nothing to apologise for."

"Well, I spoke to you like shit." I played awkwardly with my nails, avoiding eye contact.

"It's honestly fine. I just hope you're okay." Before I thought about it, I pulled him in for a hug, I'd never experienced this reaction to an apology before. No one was trying to win, we just wanted to move past this. He felt rigid for a minute before sinking into my body and hugging me back tightly. I closed my eyes and soaked in his comforting spicy cologne.

Whilst we were still in each other's arms, the door opened again and I expected to see a member of staff calling the guys to the stage. Instead, a petite, brunette model-esque woman appeared, wearing a fur coat and jeans.

"Theo?" She called towards us. Theo released me from his grip, turning towards the stranger.

"Amy, hey!" He greeted, pulling her into a hug instead. "Great to see you again."

"Thought I'd take you up on the invitation." She said once they parted. She touched his arm and my blood pressure spiked.

"I'm glad," Theo flirted. "Enjoy the show."

I looked around the room in confusion, had I missed something? Who was this girl? Locking eyes with Callum, he gave me a knowing look, like he was analysing me. Sean appeared at my side.

"If it wasn't obvious, that's the girl from last night." He said quietly into my ear and just like that, all my released tension was back at an alarming rate.

22

THEO

I wish I could say that it was due to Sean's obnoxious snoring in the bunk below that I was still awake. But the cause of my unrest was currently sleeping soundly in the bed across the aisle.

The past twenty-four hours had been a complete and utter fuckery. Why I thought it would make things simpler to bring a girl to the gig tonight, I would never know. Amelia told me to leave her alone, so that's what I had tried to do but all it did was complicate matters further.

In between moments of Amelia carrying out her usual route along the front of the crowd to take photos, I observed the two women conversing at the side of the stage whenever she would return. My mind raced between the woman who wanted me and the woman I wanted.

I tried to act normal and put on the same bravado as I did every night but I couldn't bring myself to make eyes at the camera or its operator in the same way. Although I wasn't flirting with Amelia for once, I hadn't diverted that attention to Amy either.

I pulled back the curtain of my section and looked over towards Amelia's bunk, which was shut off by her own one. Feeling disappointed that she wasn't tossing and turning too, I began to redraw the curtain. Just before it fully closed, I spotted a glow from the edge of the material.

Unlocking my phone, I texted her.

Awake?

Less than a second passed until I saw the three dots appear on screen as she typed her reply. They vanished and no response came through. A weird stab in my gut caught me off guard. *I guess she doesn't want to talk.*

The sound of her curtain opening, reignited my hope and I mirrored the action. I could barely make out her face from across the walkway of the dark bus. She offered me a small wave and I returned the gesture, my heart involuntarily warming in a dangerous way.

In an attempt not to wake my bandmates at three in the morning I typed out a message for Amelia.

Can't sleep?

Her phone lit up and illuminated her soft features as she checked the text, I watched her lips quirk up into a slight smile before she tapped in her reply.

Sofa?

I smiled and nodded towards her. The two of us jumped down from our respective bunks, trying to keep quiet. I followed Amelia through the bus towards the lounge area, flicking on the lamp as I passed.

She flopped down on the sofa, looking adorable in a matching plaid pyjama set, I realised then that I was merely wearing a pair of grey sweatpants.

"What's on your mind, Sunflower?" I asked, keeping my voice low, sitting beside her on the couch.

She released a breath, "Just can't sleep, you know how it is."

I nodded. "All too well, to be honest." I ran a hand through my hair.

We sat in silence for a second, Amelia played with one of her tight curls, seemingly deep in thought. "We're okay, aren't we?" Her voice shook.

I whipped my head towards her, shocked by the question. "Of course we are, Mils. Why wouldn't we be?" The look on Amelia's face could have shattered my heart, her chocolate eyes filled with unshed tears. "Hey hey, what's wrong?" I panicked, pulling her into my arms. She didn't resist, nuzzling into my bare skin, her body trembling with silent sobs. We sat like that for an immeasurable amount of time, I held her close while she wept, her tears sinking into my shoulder.

Eventually she calmed down enough to talk and she peered up at me through her thick lashes, her cheeks stained and eyes red. "It's just, you're the one person who always has my back and I treated you like shit." She sniffled.

"It was a tough night for you. Emotions were running high." I rubbed soothing circles on her back. "It's gonna take a lot more than shouting in the street to lose me, Sunflower." I chuckled.

"You're too good, Theo." She whispered and I couldn't help but kiss the top of her head.

"I just care about you a lot, Mils…Sorry if it's too much in your eyes." I winked at her, it was a risky joke but her lips pulled into a small smile.

"I'm glad you do. I just don't know how to show it." She said slightly, sitting up and wiping the stray tears from her face. I'd never been so proud of cheering someone up.

"How are you doing though? Have you heard from him?" I asked the burning question, unable to say the fucker's name.

She let out a sigh, trilling her lips together, "not a word but I'm okay."

I didn't know whether I fully believed her, but I'd made the mistake of pushing for information before.

"What about your date then, stud? Emma wasn't it?" She clapped her hands together with an animated look but her eyes told a different story.

"Amy," I laughed, knowing full well she remembered her name. "And what about her?"

"Will she be joining us at the next stop?"

"Jealous she'll take up all of your one-on-one Theo time? Don't worry, there's enough of me to go around, sweetheart!" I winked.

Amelia scoffed, "I'd be glad to get rid of you." She giggled and it was like music to my ears.

"Sure," I shook my head in jest, "nah, she was nice and all. But it wasn't anything serious."

And she isn't you.

"Did you…?" She elongated the question as if she felt awkward to ask but needed to know the answer.

"No." I chuckled, "I was the perfect gentleman." I discovered that night that Amy and I actually had plenty in common and under different circumstances, I may have wanted to continue getting to know her, but she didn't hold a candle to the woman sitting beside me.

Amelia nodded slightly, digesting my answer.

"Hope that answer eased your mind, Sunflower." I smirked, unsure of why she felt the need to ask the question in the first place.

She shoved my bicep, laughing to hide her embarrassment at my implication. "You wish. I was just digging for juicy gossip for the blog. I've already got a great story to share about Callum and Sean crossing swords." I narrowed my eyes in confusion. "Don't worry, I'll fill you in another time."

"Look forward to it." I laughed nervously. God only knows what those two had been getting up to unsupervised.

Amelia checked her phone before turning to me. "Right, I think it's time we try and get some sleep. The gang are meeting us in a few hours after we get to Milan and there's no way they'll excuse us for being tired."

"You're right. We've got to be in the best frame of mind for their stag and hen do's!" I agreed as she began to make her way to her bunk.

"Theo?" She turned back to face me, "thanks a lot, I needed this." She smiled so sweetly, I could have died on the spot, before disappearing back into the darkness down the hall. Thank God she didn't look back or she would have seen the embarrassing grin plastered across my face.

23

AMELIA

The high pitched screams of my friends in the lobby would have usually caused me to plug my ears and pray for it to be over. However, after nearly two months on the road, I was soaking in the noise like it was medicine.

I had been counting down the minutes until the four of us would be back together, especially after the events of Amsterdam.

As much as I didn't enjoy physical contact, when I reached them, I pulled them in and hugged them into my body.

"We've missed you so much!" Lilah exclaimed after I had finally let them go.

"I missed you all too!"

"You look amazing! Tour life suits you." Verity complimented.

"Really, Mils? You couldn't forfeit one of your band tees for Lilah's hen?" Jake joked, pecking me on top of my head as he called out the oversized t-shirt I was wearing as a dress with tights.

"I'm sorry, I didn't pack anything green, so I had to borrow this from Theo after you dropped the theme on me last minute!" I rolled my eyes, digging back at Jacob.

"Theo, hey?" Jacob waggled his eyebrows.

"We've been cramped in a tour bus for months, sharing clothes is hardly the most intimate thing that's happened." I deflected his remark, but his eyes only sparkled with further intrigue.

"Forced proximity, hot." He winked.

"Wait a minute? Intimate?!" Verity chimed in. The three pairs of eyes from my best friends burned into my skin as I tried to formulate a response.

"She looks good in it, right?" Theo appeared from behind, cutting into the conversation.

Lilah raised her eyebrows, flicking her gaze between her brother and me. I couldn't quite read her expression.

"What's up little sis?" Theo greeted, giving her a quick hug. "Where's the dreamboat?"

"At the bar with Axel, go and grab a table." Lilah instructed. Surprisingly, he didn't chat back but did as his sister requested. He was clearly giving her a pass as it was her joint celebration.

"You look incredible," I complimented Lilah who was wearing a long white satin dress with matching heels, looking like the perfect bride to be.

"Thank you, I can't believe we're finally here!" She gushed, clasping her hands together in elation.

"And only a month and a half to go until the big day!" Verity trilled excitedly.

"On that note, let's go and find your hunky hubby!" Jacob said, linking his arm with Lilah's and strolling towards the bar.

Walking into the dimly lit room, my eyes zeroed in on the three genetically blessed men sitting together. It was criminal to have that level of handsomeness around one wooden table.

Zane's eyes lit up as he spotted his blushing bride coming towards him. If this was the way he looked at her in a random hotel in Milan, I couldn't imagine how he would survive her walking down the aisle.

"You look beautiful, *mi Joya.*" Zane drawled in his Colombian accent. Lilah wrapped her arms around his neck, pressing a kiss to his cheek.

"You don't scrub up too bad yourself." She giggled.

"What are your plans tonight then boys?" Verity asked, as Axel wrapped an arm around her waist.

"My lips are sealed." Theo pretended to lock them with a key.

"So, rum and cigars at a Gentlemen's Club then?" Axel said, deadpan as he named the three most Zane-coded activities to exist.

Theo glared at him. "Way to spoil the surprise, Axel."

"What about you girls?" Axel asked, laughing off Theo's annoyance.

"It's Lilah's last rodeo!" Verity announced, producing four glittery cowboy hats from a bag I hadn't noticed. She walked along the line of us and plonked them on each of our heads. I was certain I looked completely ridiculous as it flattened my usually voluminous hair. But the giddy look on Lilah's face erased any self-consciousness, as she slipped on the Bride sash that Verity had taken from her Mary Poppins bag. She handed out the remaining accessories.

I watched Verity and Jacob don their personalised sashes laughing as I read 'Miss Chievous' on Jake's chest and 'Maid of Dishonour' on Verity's.

Before I had the chance to read my own, Theo spoke, "Miss Behaving hey? Don't do anything I wouldn't do."

"Well, that leaves the night wide open for all possibilities then, doesn't it?" I smirked.

"We'd better get going!" Jacob stated, "to Zane and Lilah!" We all repeated his words in unison and clinked our glasses together.

Hours later, we were numerous cocktails deep, covered in personalised cowboy temporary tattoos and recovering from the number of penises we had watched swinging on the stage earlier that night at a men's stripper show – think Dreamboys or Magic Mike Live but with a cast of hunky Italian men.

"That was insane, I can't believe you were pulled up on stage, Lilah!"

"I can, she's a sexy queen!" Jacob bigged her up as we prepared to take another tequila shot at the table of our VIP booth.

"Honestly, that was the most awkward moment of my life." She laughed, "I fucking loved it and I love you all!" Lilah slurred slightly.

"We love you too!" We all chorused, sinking the shots.

"Anyway, Miss Behaving," she pointed an accusatory finger at me. "What's going on with you and my brother then hey?" There was a certain glint in her eye that reassured me she wasn't asking to scold me.

"Oh yeah, there was totally a vibe!" Verity agreed, sliding closer to me on her seat.

"I agree but she's still with Mr Careless." Jacob chimed in.

"Not exactly." I admitted somewhat ashamed that I hadn't kept my friends in the loop. But given Josh and I's past and the speed in which things changed in our relationship, I could hardly keep up myself.

"Well, I'll toast to that, fuck the arsehole." Jacob raised his empty shot glass.

"Fuck the arsehole!" The girls chanted back, also raising their glasses. I couldn't help but laugh at their animated celebration.

"So, what *is* happening between you and Theo then?" Lilah repeated, gunning for information.

I didn't know how to respond, I'd hardly worked out what was going on between Theo and I myself. "Nothing. Well it *was* nothing."

"I'm sorry what, spill the beans, now!" Jacob grabbed my hand.

I flicked my eyes towards Lilah to check that she was still happy to have this conversation before continuing. "We kissed; well, he kissed me. But I didn't stop it." The copious amounts of alcohol in my system unlocked the vault where I had been keeping all this information to myself.

They sat like goldfish, mouth agape before answering in a flurry.

"When was this?" Lilah asked excitedly.

"Wow! I guess Josh is out of the picture for good then?" Verity enquired.

"Oh my God, how was it?" Jake could hardly comprehend that his dream pairing was coming into fruition - and at the detriment of Josh no less.

I took a minute to register the questions. "In Lisbon, it's complicated and it was," I paused, "good!"

The four of us screamed and for once, I joined them caught up in the hysteria. The alcohol in my system was really helping me work out what my feelings for Theo were. My guard was down for the first time and I was enjoying speaking honestly.

"Ugh, jealous!" Jake joked. "If it didn't work out with Noah, I was hoping to seduce Theo!"

"You'll be my sister-in-law!"

"Hold your horses, cowgirl!" I giggled to myself at the sound of a Theo-like saying falling from my lips. "I don't even know what we are at the moment. It's a long story and I won't bore you with the details. Tonight's about you."

"Oh fuck, I'm gonna be sick." Lilah moaned, turning a similar shade of green to our outfits.

"Shit sorry if I painted an awful mental image. I promise nothing else happened."

"No babe, too many tequilas!" She mumbled incoherently as the three of us helped Lilah to her feet.

"Come on you, let's get you back to the hotel."

24

THEO

The waitress carried over yet another tray of glasses filled with Medellin Reserve - Zane's favourite drink and placed them on the marble table.

"*Grazie mille.*" Zane thanked in perfect Italian. The woman blushed, flashing him a thousand kilo-watt smile before walking away.

"Of course you speak Italian." I chuckled, rolling my eyes. I leant back in the grand leather chair and looked around the room. I had never felt so out of place in an establishment before. The walls basically dripped with gold and the clientele likely had bank accounts bursting at the seams but for a man as rich as Zane and a star as well-known as Axel, it was the perfect place for them to kick back and relax without being disturbed.

"Congrats to Zane, the first of us to get hitched and the best damn looking groom and not to mention, to

a beautiful bride as well. Wishing you all the best, man."
Axel raised his crystal tumbler, *";Salud!"*

"Couldn't have said it better myself," I agreed, cheersing my glass with theirs.

"Thank you both and thanks for tonight." Zane replied simply, sinking his drink and placing the glass down beside the empty cigar box. "Enough about me, how's the tour been going?"

Before I had a chance to reply, Axel jumped into the conversation, "more importantly, how's the bachelor life in Europe?"

I laughed sheepishly, rubbing the back of my neck. "Nothing to report, I'm practising celibacy."

"What? The whole reason I hired your sister in the first place was so you could get your bachelor pad back, I thought you'd be relishing in the attention." Zane joked.

"Yeah, you haven't met a single girl?" Axel's disbelief was clear on his face.

"That's the problem, mate. She wasn't single."

"But from what I've heard she's not happy in her relationship." Zane responded, knowing exactly who I was referring to.

"Doesn't mean she wants me though." I sighed.

"Can we please stop speaking in code and just say Amelia?" Axel stated, speaking over me.

"What? You told him?" I accused my best friend, after previously confessing my feelings. Zane held his hands up in innocence.

"He didn't say anything, man. It's just blindingly obvious." Axel laughed. "Verity says her boyfriend is an arsehole."

"Ex-boyfriend," I corrected, "they broke up in Amsterdam. It was fucking messy!"

"That's great news." Zane shrugged.

"Perfect, now's your chance! Just ask her out, it's always worked for me in the past." Axel advised. I stared at the Adonis before me. *Yeah, I'm not surprised you've never been turned down, buddy!*

"Well, a breakup means nothing to those two, he always manages to worm his way back in." I wasn't trying to sound pathetic, but it came out that way.

"Fuck that guy! Go get your girl, T." Axel encouraged.

Hours later, we were back at the hotel, playing a round of poker from a set that Axel had bought especially for the evening.

"We've run out of ice, I'll go and get some more." I told the guys, picking up the empty bucket and heading out of the room. I was surprised to find that in this hotel, you could get ice from a large freezer in the hallway.

I rounded the corner and spotted Amelia sauntering towards me in her cowboy themed attire.

"Well Miss Sani, aren't you a sight for sore eyes." I smirked.

"Ah Mr Hart, fancy seeing you here!" She replied, stopping in front of me, her words slightly slurred.

"You're back early?" I questioned, knowing it was only around midnight.

"Lilah's sick, bless her," I was hardly surprised knowing how much of a lightweight she was. "I could say the same for you though."

"We're playing poker."

"Strip poker?" She questioned with a giggle.

"No, I'm afraid not. But maybe we could get a game in soon, just the two of us. I'm an awful player." I winked, "plus it might be a good opportunity for me to win my t-shirt back." I pinched the material on her shoulder.

"You know it looks better on me." She flirted, running her hands over the curves of her body, my eyes followed the movement hungrily. She had to be aware of the effect she was having on me.

"No arguments there, Sunflower." I growled; my voice low with desire. "But *this* looks better on me." I took off her cowboy hat and put it on my head.

"Sure you wanna do that?" She raised her eyebrows. I pulled a face in confusion as she closed the space between us. "You know the saying? Wear the hat, ride the cowboy." Her sweet scent dizzied my senses from the proximity and her voice dripped with seduction.

I was speechless.

Before I could retort with a witty remark, she grabbed the hat and walked away, leaving me insanely horny and dangerously hard.

25

THEO

It had been a week since the hen and stag and neither myself or Amelia had addressed the obvious flirting in the corridor. I assumed that she had forgotten all about it, thanks to the alcohol, but I couldn't say the same for myself. The sound of her voice coated with lust was all I could focus on night after night as I replayed the interaction.

And tonight, as I watched her pacing along the front of the stage the image was still crystal clear. I also noticed this evening that she wore a top that showed more cleavage than usual and my mind raced on overdrive.

Now as the crowds were leaving and the lights had been turned off, we were back in the hotel and I was desperate to sink a post-show pint, as usual.

"Gonna give this one a miss tonight boys, I'm exhausted," Finn declined, stretching his arms out. "I'll make the next one."

"Ah well if not everyone's going, Sean why don't we start that show you mentioned on the bus?" Callum said, directing his attention to our lead singer.

"Sure thing bro," Sean fist-bumped him and they began to head back up to our suites.

"Don't tell me you're gonna bail too?" I cocked an eyebrow towards Amelia who still had her camera hung around her neck.

"I'm pretty tired-" She began, trying to let me down gently.

"Come on, Sunflower. You know I'm the most fun one anyway, we don't need those three bores!" I retorted, cutting her sentence off before she could finish declining the invitation.

"Okay, I'll make you a deal." She held her chin in her hand, "I'll stay for one and we'll have it in the hotel bar."

"You drive a hard bargain, but deal."

Three drinks later, Amelia and I had lost track of time talking about everything and nothing.

"Thanks for begging me to come out tonight, I needed this." Amelia smiled, fiddling with the stem of her cocktail glass.

"Hey, enough of the 'begged', please!" I laughed, although I *would* have fucking begged her if that's what it took.

She giggled, "you know it's true." My jaw clenched as I watched her lick the sugar off the rim of her cosmo. There is no way she didn't know what she was doing to me.

A moment of silence fell between us, my mind swimming with less than appropriate thoughts.

"Theo?" Amelia broke me out of my fantasy, her big brown eyes blinking at me from across the bar table. "Can I ask you something?"

"Anything." My heart thudded in my chest at what it could be, she looked almost nervous. Instinctively, I reached across and offered her my hand, she took it gingerly before taking a deep breath.

"Josh messaged me…" I felt my whole body tense and I tried with all my might to not roll my eyes. I bit my tongue as I waited for what felt like an eternity for her to continue. "He wants to fly out to Berlin to meet and talk things through."

"Sounds romantic. So which one of his friends is having a birthday trip to Germany then?" I replied sarcastically. Amelia didn't laugh. "I assume you told him no?"

She chewed her lip, as if searching for the words to say, "I've never seen him this apologetic."

"What? More than the last time? Or the ten times before?" I couldn't stop myself. My opinions spilled out of me without control. I let go of her hand and ran mine through my hair.

"He's complicated; we've been through a lot together." She defended, recoiling into herself slightly as I raised my voice.

"Yeah, a lot of shit that *he's* put you through!" The alcohol in my system bolstered my confidence.

"Theo? Why are you being like this?"

"Because I'm sick of sitting back and watching you let yourself be treated like crap!" I threw my hands up in exasperation, leaning back in my chair.

"You don't understand."

"I understand that for the past six years he's lied to you, betrayed you, manipulated you, not to mention somehow convinced you that he's all you deserve." Amelia sat still while I ran my mouth. "But it's not, you are worthy of so much more. You deserve someone who loses sleep just to stay up talking on the phone, who would travel across the world to see you for just five minutes. Someone who notices the small details about you, the way your eyes light up when you talk about music, the way your nose crinkles when you laugh wholeheartedly, the way you look away and play with your hair when you're shy. Amelia, you deserve someone who would steal your breath away and give you butterflies-"

"That's a great fantasy, Theo," She cut me off abruptly. "But in reality, who's going to treat me like that?"

"I would."

26

AMELIA

"What?" I must have misunderstood, but Theo was looking at me with such sincerity my heart stuttered.

"You heard me, Mils."

"But, you can't mean tha-"

"Of course I do." He interrupted. "There's nothing I wouldn't do for you, Amelia." His earnest eyes bored into mine as he bared his soul.

"Why are you saying all of this? You must be drunk." I protested, feeling vulnerable, unwilling to let myself believe his confession - one that I had wanted him to say for so long. "Theo, I can't believe this."

"I know I've overstepped, and I know we're just friends but I needed you to understand that there's more out there than fucking Josh." He let out an exhale. "I just had to tell you how I feel."

He shuffled awkwardly in his seat, as words failed me. "On that revelation, I'll catch ya later, Sunflower." Theo stood and began to walk past me.

"Theo!" I called, finally finding my voice. He was standing one step away. I stood to face him and without taking a moment to second guess myself, pulled his body to mine, crashing my lips to his.

He stilled for a moment before melting into me. Moving his mouth in time with mine.

"Amelia," he breathed against my lips saturated with so much need it was almost desperate, which only ignited the fire in my belly further.

His hands snaked their way around my waist, leaving goosebumps in their wake as my fingers wound into his hair, pulling him to me hungrily. I was a ball of lust, every nerve ending alight with desire, every inhibition gone, every thought of the outside world non-existent. All I could focus on was Theo as his touch seared into my skin.

"Let's get out of here." I whispered, barely believing the words were coming out of my mouth.

"Your room or mine, Sunflower?" His breath ghosted over my lips in the split second they were apart.

"Anywhere, I just need you." My voice wobbled with desperation, I hardly recognised myself.

We were a blur of tangled limbs and carnal passion as we somehow made it to the tenth floor. I barely had time to register my surroundings before my back hit the solid wood of Theo's hotel door.

"Do you have any idea how crazy you have been driving me, Amelia?" He growled and I shivered from the dominance in his voice. I hated to admit it, but I had imagined how he'd be in a situation like this on more than one occasion, and he was certainly surpassing expectations. "I asked you a question, Sunflower."

My mind blanked for a second as I tried to remember how to function. "Wh-what?" I stuttered - failing. This wasn't the Theo I was used to but I loved it

He pulled back and leant a hand against the door above me. A smirk pulled at his lips. "Actually, I'd rather know how much I have been driving *you* crazy?"

I panicked, mulling over my response for a second or two. Should I give the shy answer or the honest one?

I never considered myself as a liar. "Too much."

As soon as the confession left my mouth it was like a switch flicked in him, suddenly he whipped me into his arms and carried me across the room. I let out a squeal as he dropped me onto the bed.

Watching in awe as the stunning man crawled above me, hair messed from my frantic touch, lips swollen from my kiss and pupils dilated with lust.

As he began to travel downwards, my fingers curled around the hem of his shirt and pulled it over his head with ease. A smug chuckle rumbled through his chest as I grazed my eyes over the deep lines of his abs. I couldn't help but trail a hand over his bare stomach, my mouth watered. I had *never* been with a man like this before.

He undid the button of my jeans and began sliding the denim material down my legs, I lifted my hips eagerly. "You're so ready for me, aren't you?"

I whimpered, pathetically as he hooked his fingers around the lace of my underwear, removing them completely. I laid there, bare and ready for him. The air against my wet pussy caused me to shiver and whine needily. I'd never needed to be touched so badly. "I've waited years for this, Amelia. I'm going to take my sweet time with you." He purred, in response to the needy noises falling from my lips.

He shook his head almost in disbelief before reaching a hand between my thighs. "God, you're so fucking wet." I hadn't realised how turned on I was in the midst of it all. It was like I hadn't let myself admit it until now, almost as if I ignored it, there was a chance it would go away. But now, with Theo mere inches from my begging core, it was impossible to deny how much I had always wanted him.

He flicked his gaze to me and moved his mouth towards my clit. I grabbed his chin and angled his face to meet my eye line. "Don't be offended, if I don't...you know." I felt my cheeks heat with embarrassment. In six years with Josh I had never been able to orgasm. I had come to the realisation that it was simply something I wasn't able to do in front of other people and I didn't want to ruin this moment with Theo, by making him feel bad, when I inevitably didn't climax.

"Oh yeah? Let's see about that, Sunflower." Theo grinned a devilish smile, "I like a challenge." With that he dived in.

His tongue swirled eagerly around my sensitive bud, causing fireworks to shoot along every nerve. I clamped my eyes shut as I lost myself in the blissful sensation.

"Look at me." He demanded between licks. I obeyed and forced my eyelids back open to see his hazel eyes staring at me from between my legs. I could see how much he was enjoying it from his stare alone. "Good girl."

I groaned involuntarily at the praise. As he slipped two fingers inside me, my gasp quickly transformed into a moan. "Theo." I breathed, as he continued to lick my clit hungrily and the pressure built in my lower abdomen. I stared down at him, mesmerized by the vision before me, although I couldn't see his mouth, I felt every single movement and it was mind blowing.

The euphoria built quickly at the bottom of my spine. I recognised the feeling but had never experienced this at the hands - or in this case mouth - of another person. "Theo, I-I." Before I could finish the thought, a crash of ecstasy swept over me, knocking me off course. My limbs tingled, my back arched and my vision blurred as I came on his tongue. I shuddered through the best orgasm of my life, genuinely feeling like I'd had an out of body experience. Once I had regained some level of control over my limbs, I leant up onto my elbows, looking at the man before me, with bleary eyes. "What the fuck." I panted, dumbfounded by what had just happened. No one had ever done that to me before.

"So, who's keeping count?" He smirked, wiping his face with his fingers before popping his thumb in his mouth, savouring the taste of me.

"Keeping count?" I asked, barely coherent.

"Of how many times I make you come tonight." My breath hitched. "So, how many was that, Sunflower?"

I swallowed past the dry lump in my throat. "One."

"That's my girl."

Before I had time to refocus my thoughts, Theo flipped me over, so I was flat on the mattress. He leant over me, his mouth lining up with my ear before he slid his fingers back inside me and curled them to meet my most sensitive spot. I cried out, unable to hold back. "You taste so good, Amelia, I already miss your cunt on my tongue."

He began pumping into me with intense vigour. My brain scrambled as I buried my face into the duvet. The only sound was the sweet nothings he whispered into my ear as my second orgasm hit me with full force.

"What number was that?" He growled into the shell of my ear. I shivered.

"Two."

My response was barely audible. As I came down from my high, I heard the sound of plastic ripping before Theo slid a condom onto his dick. I turned back to take in the God behind me.

Who would have thought that under the baggy band tees and faded jeans, were washboard abs and a seven-inch cock!

"You make me so hard, Amelia."

I whimpered in anticipation. His strong hands grabbed my hips and lifted me onto all fours. I couldn't speak. I was begging pathetically for him, pushing back against him hoping for any form of friction.

He took my silence as admission and slammed into me. I threw my head back automatically. The stretch I felt from him was incredible. I'd never felt so full.

"God, your pussy feels so fucking tight." He held onto my hips as he mercilessly thrust into me. I felt a sharp pain against my arse as he spanked me and it bloomed into pleasure. "Do you like that, Sunflower?" He asked. The surge of adrenaline that coursed through my veins was like nothing I had felt before. I wanted more, more. I never wanted this feeling to end.

"Yes, Theo, you feel so good." I almost sobbed, "so fucking good." My words spurred him on and I melted into the sensation. Just like before, tension coiled at the base of my spine.

I pushed my hips back against his groin as his full length hit a point impossibly deep.

"Fuck, Theo!" I exclaimed. The elation fizzed to the ends of my fingers and toes as yet another mind-altering climax ricocheted through my body. Theo worked me through my third orgasm, my moans echoing around the room.

"Well?" He questioned with a cocky tone.

"Three."

Once I had come down from my high I felt him pull out of me slowly. I slumped forward before he flipped me over once again, positioning himself back between my legs. I stared up at him, taken aback by his beauty.

"You are so beautiful, Mils." He placed a soft kiss on my lips. "What do you say? One more, Sunflower?" I nodded meekly, "but I want to see all of you." He began to roll up my t-shirt, as it peaked over my breasts, self-consciousness flooded my brain. It took everything in my power not to get up, turn the light off and hide in the darkness but the way Theo's eyes were exploring my torso, dispelled all of my anxieties.

I couldn't handle the intensity of his stare and pulled his face to mine, claiming his lips with my own. Our tongues fought for dominance as I felt the head of his cock press against my pussy.

"How badly do you want it?" Theo whispered. "Hm?"

"Stop playing." I whined. He was so close, yet agonisingly far.

"Come on, Amelia. One admission and I'll make you come harder than ever."

I'd never been one to plead but I had never wanted something so badly. Infact it wasn't a want, it was a *need*. "Fuck me, Theo. Please."

"Okay, no need to beg." He winked; a cocky smile pulled at his lips. Painfully slowly, he slid his cock into me and began to thrust at a rhythmic pace. He never broke eye contact, worshipping me with his gaze.

"Fuck, I can't believe this is real." He breathed, barely making a sound. I grabbed the back of his arms as his rhythm picked up, each thrust sparking blinding pleasure through me.

I dug my nails into his biceps, "I'm going to co-" before I could finish the sentence a mind shattering orgasm ripped through my body. I felt Theo twitch inside me as he groaned, releasing into the condom before collapsing on top of me. I felt overcome with emotion at what we had just done and the pleasure I had just experienced.

Once the dust settled, we were a sweaty pile of unsaid words and post-orgasmic bliss. Theo rolled off me and pulled me into his arms.

"God, Theo. that was-"

He held his hand up, shushing me. "Number?"

I giggled, "four."

27

THEO

I awoke to the feeling of Amelia shuffling in her sleep and pulled her closer, her bare back flattening against my chest. Her curly hair tickled my nose as I snuggled into her. I half imagined that I would open my eyes this morning to find that I was alone in my hotel room and last night had been a wishful, albeit vivid, dream. But finding Amelia, sleeping soundly to my side, was a feeling I could definitely get used to.

"Morning, Sunflower," I said as her eyes flicked open and she turned towards me. "Sorry if I woke you."

"You didn't," she yawned before a smile pulled at her full lips. "Besides, this is a nice way to wake up, no apologies necessary." My heart warmed and a tension I didn't realise I was holding released from my muscles, at the reassurance Amelia was happy in my arms. I pressed a kiss to her forehead and she let out a peaceful sigh.

"How are you?" I asked.

She let out a breathy giggle, "exhausted!" An uncontrolled laugh escaped from me at her unexpected answer. "You know, no one has ever made me come before."

"Really?" The confession caught me off guard but my ego swelled with pride. The way she was blinking up at me proved she wasn't lying. "So, you've never orgasmed before?"

She rolled her eyes, "I'm a thirty-one-year-old woman, Theo. Of course I've orgasmed before." She tapped my bare chest playfully, "just never with a partner." She confirmed coyly. The thought of Amelia getting herself off caused a rush of blood to shoot to my dick.

"Well, the honour was all mine." I winked at her. "If you need a helping hand again, you know where to find me."

"Fuck off, Theo." She laughed, jokingly pushing me away.

"Come here you." I pulled her closer and breathed in her sweet scent. I held her in my arms, it was crazy that it had taken us so long to reach this point, especially given how right it felt. Seeing Amelia so relaxed and content made me happier than I could've ever imagined, especially given how many times I'd seen her down or upset over the past few years. "Shall we address the elephant in the room?"

"What's that?" She responded, looking at me from under her lashes.

"What time are you meeting Josh?" I joked, a chuckle rumbled in my chest at the thought of that dickhead thinking he was days away from reeling her back in. I wished I could be there to watch the look on his face when he realised the door was shut for good.

Amelia grimaced before furrowing her brow. "Okay, okay, bad joke." I held up my hands in surrender.

She slipped out of my grasp, reaching across the bed to pick up her phone from my side table. As the screen illuminated, Josh's name caught my eye.

"Ugh, what a mess." Amelia groaned, facing the phone towards me.

> I'm looking at flights now, boo.
> Say the word and I'll be there.

Bless him. "Surely you're going to tell him not to come right?" I tried to mask the pathetic question with fake bravado but I had to ask. I'd wanted her for years and here she was, finally mine. I wasn't going to let that go easily.

"Yes, no. I don't know." She sighed deeply, dropping the phone onto the mattress and covering her face with her hands.

"What's the confusion?" I sat up onto my elbow, trying to keep my tone light but tension coiled in my stomach.

"Obviously I'm going to tell him not to come," she uncovered her face, "but the last thing I wanted was to break up with him, jump into bed with you and become just another notch on your bedpost. I know your reputation."

The assumption hurt more than I anticipated. Amelia knew I hadn't been sleeping around so the jab stung. "Is that really what you think you are to me?"

Her face softened as if the stress was being released from her body, "no." She let out a breath, "I know you care about me."

I didn't have the words to confirm how true that statement was, instead I nodded, glad she understood our situation. Although, I could tell she was fighting against her own insecurities.

"And for the record, I would never have slept with you if I had any intention of getting back together with Josh."

28

AMELIA

The look of happiness on Theo's face at my confirmation, compelled me to take his jaw in my hands and pull him forward for a kiss. There was no need for his doubts or concerns. I could see through his jokes and light heartedness that he was concerned this was just rebound sex.

I could wholeheartedly say it wasn't. I wasn't quite sure how to put what this was into words but it was the farthest thing from rebound sex. It was the BEST SEX EVER!

Theo's hands roamed my naked torso, our breaths became heavier and wetness pooled between my legs. I knew that if I didn't break this up now, we wouldn't be leaving this hotel room today - and I'd never been to Rome before. As tempting as being holed up with Theo was, pizza was calling! "I'm going to get in the shower, be right back!"

He playfully slapped my backside as I slid out from under the covers and darted to the bathroom, grabbing my discarded clothes from the night before as I went.

Once I was alone, I unlocked my phone which I had grabbed enroute and opened Josh's message.

I stared at it for a minute, pondering my words. Josh had been my constant for six years and sending this text would confirm that this truly was the final break up.

Although there was a small part of me that was sad, I knew overwhelmingly, this was what I wanted and a future, without him, was the right path to go down.

I typed back my reply telling him not to meet me in Berlin and that it was over for good. Exhaling a deep breath, I re-read the message before hitting send. I locked my phone, not wanting to see a reply.

Placing the phone on the counter of the sink, I looked up to see my reflection in the mirror and barely recognised myself. I couldn't help but laugh out loud.

Who knew all I needed to look my best were four orgasms and a good night's sleep in an emperor bed that felt like a cloud, cuddled up to a fit guitarist!

I shook my head and walked into the huge shower, turning on the water that was the perfect temperature. I closed my eyes in the stream of droplets and let them cascade over me as visions of last night with Theo played on a loop. The way his touch seared my skin, the way he expertly worked me towards *multiple* orgasms. I clenched my thighs together as the memories became so vivid it was almost as if he was here with me.

The feeling of soft lips on my neck brought me out of my daydream.

"Thinking about me, Sunflower?" He growled into my ear as he slipped his hand around my waist, pulling me against his raging erection. I melted into his touch and let out a low moan as his fingers started to move along my thighs towards my already wet core.

"How did you know?" I breathed.

He dipped a finger inside me and groaned, "you're soaking wet, baby." He nipped my earlobe and I melted against him.

He slowly began to circle my clit, pleasure spreading like wildfire through my body.

"Theo, I'm trying to shower." I giggled, my protest sounded weak to my own ears as I silently willed him not to stop.

"Let me help." He moved his hand away and before I could register what he was doing, I felt the warm pressure of water against my core. A loud moan escaped my lips.

"Fuck." He held the shower head against me, the stream of warm water on my sensitive clit was unlike anything I'd felt before. He wrapped his free hand around my wet curls and pulled my head back on his shoulder. The water from the rainfall shower head above poured over us as Theo kissed and nibbled my neck in a way that was almost certainly going to leave a mark but in that moment I didn't care. I was turned on by the thought of being branded by him.

"You look so fucking good, Sunflower. With the water running over your perfect tits." His voice quivered with barely restrained need, the head of his cock painfully hard against my backside. He let go of my hair and trailed a hand over my torso towards my breast. He rubbed my peaked nipple between his thumb and forefinger as he rotated the jets of the shower against my clit.

"How are you so good at this?" I whispered. "Lots of practice?" It was a joke that I hoped didn't ruin the moment. He chuckled, causing every hair on my body to stand further on edge.

"Believe me, this is special treatment. I've been dreaming of this," he spoke softly into my ear as I began to see stars. The relentless stimulation skyrocketed me towards climax.

My legs began to tremble, if it weren't for Theo holding me up I would have crumbled to the floor. My breathing became frantic and my moans echoed around the cubicle. Warm heat coiled at the base of my spine, becoming almost unbearable as my orgasm approached rapidly.

"Good girl," Theo complimented. Although I couldn't see his reaction, I could visualise the smirk on his face, from the sound of his words.

His hand travelled from my chest towards my jaw, tilting my face towards him, "look at me when you come, baby." My vision was bleary but the way Theo was staring at me, water droplets in his hair and lashes, lip pulled between his teeth, concentrating on my pleasure alone, tipped me over the edge. I came long and hard, crying out louder than ever before. Theo's hand moved from my jaw and clamped over my mouth, so the rest of the hotel guests didn't complain.

My legs shook and Theo held me up as the waves of euphoria rippled through every nerve ending. Frantically I pushed the shower head away from my dripping core, the sensation unbearable all of a sudden.

"Such a good fucking girl for me, Amelia." He whispered, kissing the side of my neck once again. "I'll leave you alone now." He left the room as if he hadn't just reduced me to a mess.

I quickly showered and dried myself on shaky legs, using one of the largest and softest towels I had ever used before redressing. Opening the door to the bathroom, I was surprised to find Theo fully dressed, lying against the pillows on his bed.

"I'll see you later than I guess?" I said sheepishly, feeling awkward suddenly, as if I'd outstayed my welcome.

"Are you ditching me?" He looked up, surprised.

"What? No? I just thought-"

"Well, you thought wrong Amelia. I'm taking you out on a proper date." He cut me off. I could feel the warmth heating my cheeks at the prospect of a romantic outing with him.

"Oh okay," The offer was unexpected, I knew he had insisted his feelings for me ran deep. But it was hard to imagine someone like him wanted someone like me.

"Wow, don't get too excited!" Theo responded sarcastically, laughing slightly.

"Oh, sorry," I giggled, awkwardly. "I just need to go and get some new clothes; these are gross from the gig!"

"Let's go then, Sunflower." Theo jumped up from the bed, slung on his jacket and grabbed his keycard before we popped back to my room.

It took much longer than I had anticipated to change into a new set of clothes. However, I wanted to look my best for this outing. I was second-guessing everything and scrutinising every decision. We had spent lots of time together in the past, but now with the added layer of confirmed attraction, my nerves were multiplying!

29

THEO

The sun beating down on me, a light breeze in my hair, the smell of restaurants all around and the most beautiful girl I'd ever seen on my arm: life didn't get much better than this.

"Are we going anywhere in particular or just wandering around until we find something?" Amelia questioned, looking at the collection of cafes that lined the streets.

"I'm offended! Don't you remember the date I planned for us in Lisbon?" I asked, squeezing her hand in mine.

"That wasn't a date." Amelia protested, though I could see her trying to suppress a smile.

"Whatever you say, Sunflower. Felt like a date to me." I winked and she rolled her eyes, that smile breaking free and spreading across her gorgeous face.

I led Amelia down the busy street, taking in the grand buildings around us as we made our way to the restaurant I had booked this morning.

"Whoa, it's bigger than I expected!" Amelia gushed looking at the famous Roman landmark.

"The Colosseum or me?" I smirked.

She turned her attention to me and shot daggers before simply replying, "both."

It was my fault for asking the question, but I immediately felt blood rush to my groin and silently cursed myself for always having my mind in the gutter. I laughed and shook my head attempting to keep things PG.

We continued down the road until I stopped outside a plain entranceway. "After you." I let go of her hand and opened the door. Amelia began to walk into the unassuming hallway. I joined her at the end of the aisle and pressed the button to call the elevator.

As we rode the lift, I looked at her perfect face. She didn't show it but I was certain she was confused why I had brought her to this particular place which seemed so basic in comparison to the other impressively decorated restaurants further along the journey.

The doors opened to reveal one of the most beautiful dining rooms I had ever seen. There was a sea of immaculately laid tables, with silverware glinting as the sun reflected off it through the high windows. Gold accents decorated the walls and pillars throughout the room, leading to an impressive balcony. To top it off, we were the only people dining. Another perk of being a rockstar: being able to hire out sought after venues at a moment's notice!

The maître d' greeted us and guided us through to the terrace, where a single table had already been laid with a bottle of sparkling wine and a basket of bread.

I pulled Amelia's chair out for her as she took a seat, before shuffling my own chair under the table, opposite.

Amelia's eyes were like saucers as she looked around. "This is incredible." She breathed, barely audible. I watched as her gaze darted between the extravagant interior and the magnificent view of the Colosseum which we were overlooking.

"Do you like it?" I asked, taking her hand across the table.

"I don't know what to say." She stuttered, eyes welling up. "Sorry," she wiped them before any tears could fall, "this is just the nicest thing anyone's ever done for me. Well, except you in Lisbon of course, but I guess what I'm trying to say is thank you."

"You deserve the world, Amelia. And I will always show you that." I squeezed her hand in mine, my heart beaming that I could make her so happy, while simultaneously aching at the fact she had felt so underappreciated for so long.

"I hope you don't mind but I ordered a selection of bits ahead." As I spoke, the waiters carried over a margherita pizza, bowl of carbonara and a board of Italian meats and cheeses.

"Not at all, looks like you have amazing taste!" Amelia responded, looking eagerly at the food that was now laid out on our table.

We began to tuck into the meal which was utterly delicious! "So, tell me Amelia, I know you love music journalism but what is your ultimate dream?"

"It sounds so silly," she began, self-doubt already coating her words as if she was reciting a certain someone's previously voiced opinion. Although I was yet to find out what her goal was, I was convinced it was anything but silly and that Amelia could achieve anything she put her mind to. "I've always dreamt of starting my own record label to give smaller bands a chance. Much like an extension of my blog but obviously on a much larger and more expensive scale!" She avoided eye contact with me, as if not waiting to see my initial reaction.

"Amelia, that is a great dream! I can't wait to see that come to fruition in the future. You'll help so many amazing artists, I'm sure. Got any names in mind?"

Her eyes lit up at my enthusiasm as I encouraged her to continue, "well, the obvious would be to use the blog title. So, Under The Radar Records but I'm always on the lookout for the perfect one!"

"That sounds pretty perfect to me, Sunflower." I smiled what I could only imagine was a goofy grin but I loved seeing her like this. So enthusiastic and excited.

"What about you, superstar? I guess you're already living your dreams?" She said, twirling her fork in the pasta before taking a bite.

"Yeah, I'm pretty lucky, but my main dream, as soppy as it sounds, is to have a family of my own. I have Lilah of course,"

"And Zane," she added jokingly.

"Yes, who could forget that handsome son-of-a-bitch," I winked, "but it's just the two of us and I want to build a family where my kids have two parents and a loving home. Something Lilah and I unfortunately didn't get."

Amelia's face sobered at the realisation of my words. "I don't know much about what happened, but Lilah has told me some info over the years. You guys didn't deserve all of that heartbreak."

"Thanks," I smiled awkwardly. "So yeah, that's my biggest dream but also my biggest fear. I don't know much about him, but I'm terrified of ending up like my own dad." *A waste of space loser who deserts his children…*

Amelia reached out across the table and squeezed my hand. "Theo, I don't need to have met your dad to know that you are *nothing* like him. I've never met anyone like you before." The last sentence came out as a whisper and I felt my heart warm.

"Ah really?" I smirked, lightening the mood, "in what way?"

She rolled her eyes and smiled back at me, "I'm not just going to sit here and boost your ego, Theo." A giggle escaped her lips, "but you're not the same person."

I hummed half-heartedly in agreement. It was insane to think how much someone who I hadn't seen since I was five could have such a hold on me still. I would never understand how he could abandon us; Lilah and I were so small. Although it hurt, I was lucky to still grow up with a loving mother who always did her best.

"Anyway, enough about my dysfunctional family, tell me about yours!" I implored, not caring to discuss the deadbeat any longer.

"Erm, my family are pretty great." She responded, looking like she was trying not to gloat after my sob story. "I have a small family like yours, just me, Mum and Dad. We've always been really close, probably 'cos I'm an only child."

I smiled at her. "They sound great, Mils." The thought of a young, curly haired Amelia running around her childhood home with her mother and father made my chest swell. "I'd love to meet them one day."

"Yeah, they'd love you I reckon." She gazed past me as if imagining the scene in her head and smiled, before her expression turned anxious. "Don't take this badly, but I really don't want to get played around again, Theo, so I want to take things slow between us."

The thought that Amelia didn't want to shout this from the rooftops, like I did, stung initially however I had to remind myself about the six years of shit she had gone through and knew this was her insecurities and not her opinion of me.

"If that's what you want, then I'm onboard. Just tell me what you need."

"Trust me, Theo, I want this, I just want to keep it between us at the moment." She chewed on her bottom lip. "Is that okay?"

I reached across the table and took her hand, "as far as I'm concerned I'm yours and only yours so I'll wait as long as you need."

****

Awake?

Sofa.

Amelia and I hopped down from our respective bunks and congregated on the couch, at the back of the bus. Since deciding not to tell my bandmates, we had to find time to be together without arousing suspicion whenever we could.

It pained me to say goodnight to her and crawl into separate bunks, not being able to pull her closer and feel her body against mine. I had waited too long to have only held her for one night. But we would be in Berlin soon and back in the privacy of a hotel, being able to sneak around to our heart's content.

I padded behind Amelia as she made her way towards the seating area, before she could sit down, I wrapped my arms around her waist and tackled her to the cushions in a bear hug. She tried to hold in her laughter to remain inconspicuous as we crashed into the fabric. "Theo, what are you doing?" She giggled.

"Missed ya. It's not fair that we have to sleep in separate beds. I feel like a teenager." I nuzzled my face into the side of her neck and placed a kiss just above her collarbone. Her breath caught and a smug smile pulled at my lips.

"Oh yeah? What did you miss about me?" There was a seductive edge to her usually dry tone, which made my hairs stand on end.

I ran my nose along the edge of her jaw before placing a kiss there. "I missed the feeling of your skin under my fingertips and the way your body reacts to mine." I trailed a hand along her torso, noticing the way her breathing changed as my fingers brushed the side of her breast. "I can't wait to be alone with you again." I spoke in a hushed tone as I twirled one of her curls between my fingers. My cock throbbed with the mental images of Amelia, naked, begging for me. I wished I could take her now and fuck her to oblivion on this sofa.

"We *are* alone." She said simply, looking around the room to confirm it was just the two of us in the darkness. Her words were a shot of adrenaline to my balls.

"We can't." I swallowed past the lump in my throat as she began to move her hand down my bare chest. Fuck she was making this so much harder for me…in every sense of the word!

"Of course we can." She shuffled until she was straddling me. I was certain she could feel the obnoxious bulge in my jogging bottoms.

"Amelia." The warning sounded strained. She began to rock her hips, pushing her groin against my own. *Fuck, this is torture.*

"Come on, Theo. I didn't take you for a scaredy-cat." She leant down and trailed open-mouthed kisses down my neck and across my chest. I gripped the edge of the couch, trying not to look at the vixen in front of me as she slid off my lap onto her knees.

"You're the one who wanted to keep it a secret." I groaned, doing everything in my power to hold back. Her hot breath was dangerously close to the hem of my trousers and I imagined how it would feel to slip my dick into her eager little mouth.

"You better be quiet then." She smirked, sliding my clothes down to reveal my erection, already glistening with pre-cum. She held up a finger in a 'shh' motion, the moonlight illuminated the action which threatened to knock me over the edge before her mouth enveloped the tip of my cock.

I clenched my jaw tightly, trying to avoid moaning too loudly and waking up the three sound asleep musicians metres away. (And alerting the driver!) The only thing preventing us from being caught was a measly curtain.

"God, Sunflower. How could I ever say no to you?" I groaned and wrapped my hand around the base of her ponytail, guiding her movements as her lips glided along the length of me. She moaned enthusiastically, encouraging me to tighten the hold I had on her hair.

Peering down at her was almost too much, her big brown eyes shone up at me filled with such adoration and determination to bring me pleasure, causing the familiar pressure to build at the base of my spine. There was no way I was going to come without being inside of her.

Abruptly I pulled her mouth away from me. She pouted, a string of spit still connecting her swollen lips to my swollen head.

"Don't give me that look, Amelia." I purred. "I know you're just as desperate to come as I am, from the way you're clenching your thighs together." She was almost panting from arousal, I could only imagine how sopping wet her cunt would be.

I leant across to a drawer beside the sofa and retrieved a condom. She quirked an eyebrow. "I know it's pig-headed but four boys on the road, safety first, right?" I chuckled, ripping the plastic and sliding it onto my cock. I wrapped my arms around Amelia, who was still kneeling on the floor and lifted her easily onto my lap. She wasn't wearing any underwear beneath her nightdress so I lowered her onto my length.

"Fuck!" She cried out. I clamped my hand over my mouth.

"Quiet, remember?" I winked at her and began pounding deep into her core, hitting her g-spot with every thrust. Amelia squeezed her eyes shut, trying with all her might not to scream and give the game away.

I kept my hand covering her lips, muffling whatever sound escaped. Watching her ride my cock was like nothing I had ever experienced before. The tight pink satin clung to her breasts, bouncing vigorously with every movement, focusing my attention on her erect nipples.

Instinctively, my free hand travelled beneath the material, finding the peaked bud and pinching it between my finger and thumb.

Amelia squeaked and her eyelids flew open, looking panicked that she wasn't going to be able to keep quiet through her climax.

"That's it, Sunflower. Come all over my cock for me." I whispered, bringing my hand back down to her hip and bouncing her harder on me. "Good girl, keep nice and quiet." I encouraged. I was in awe as I watched the euphoria spread across her face, her pussy rippled around me and my own orgasm crashed over in full force. Both of us gasped for air, desperately trying not to scream the bus awake as pleasure ripped through our bodies.

Once I came down from my high, I removed my other hand from her mouth and she let out a breathy laugh. "Only one this time?" She joked.

A surprised chuckle escaped my lips at her audacity. "Don't challenge me, Sunflower." I warned as she moved from on top of me to snuggle into my side. "You and I both know, if I give you any more of those, we'll definitely be waking up the boys." She giggled and I pressed a kiss to the side of her head.

We lay there in silence, soaking in the post-orgasmic bliss and simplicity of being in each other's arms, dreading the moment we had to separate and go back to being 'just friends' to the rest of the world.

30

AMELIA

"Hey babe, how's it going? Where are you?" Jake bellowed through my phone screen as his face appeared. It had only been a couple of weeks since we had all met up for Lilah's hen in Milan, but the King of Gossip always liked to be kept up to date with the goings on in our lives.

"It's great. We're in Berlin, it's the final show of the first leg of the tour so I think the vibe will be amazing. I can already hear the crowds chanting from outside the venue." I responded, talking louder than I usually would as the band warmed up their instruments on stage. Jake had called during the soundcheck for tonight. When I was free, I tried to come down and document it for the blog, plus I enjoyed being the only audience member for a change!

"Awesome!"

"How's Noah?" I asked, eager to hear about the two lovebirds.

"We're all settled into the flat, I can't wait to have you guys over for movie night!" He virtually gave me a quick tour of their new abode.

"Oh, Jacob, it looks so lovely! Let's arrange a date with the girls for when I'm home." I replied animatedly, being on the road had really made me appreciate my best friends.

"For sure." His expression became serious, "now I'm scared to ask but please tell me that you and Josh are still in your 'off' phase?"

I paused for a moment, so much had happened since the last time I saw Jake. Josh was barely a thought in my head anymore. "Firmly off."

"Thank the lord!" He laughed, throwing a hand up in the air. "Good riddance. How's my fave, Theo, doing?"

As if on cue, Theo called through the microphone, "is that Jake? Hey mate!"

I turned back from looking at Theo to see Jacob's reaction. I could have sworn he blushed. Even digitally, Theo could make people hot under the collar.

"You fucked him." The accusation drew me out of my daydream as I began to stutter a denial. "Don't lie to me, Mils. You fucked him. And he was *good*."

I hurriedly walked further into the corner of the auditorium, "be quiet or I'll fucking mute you." I laughed.

"Oh, so it's a dirty little secret then. That's all the confirmation I needed." He winked through the phone. "Was it good though?" He repeated. It would seem there was no avoiding it.

As much as I wanted to keep it quiet, having Jacob know the truth was quite exciting!

"Oh my God, Jacob, if only you knew how good!" I whispered, my eyes basically rolling back in my head at the memories of Theo alone!

"I'm happy for you, girl. It's about time you got some good dick." I usually wouldn't have appreciated his vulgar language but this time I had to agree with him.

"Yeah, let's just say Josh is *not* on my mind right now."

"I want all the gory details, hun. I've been waiting for this for years. You can't hold back on me now." He propped his phone up on the side and clapped his hands together, ready for some juicy gossip.

"I'd love to share, Jake, but no one here knows so we will have to catch up later." I heard the final song of the set come to an end and knew it was only a matter of time before the band would vacate the stage. "I've got to dash; promise I'll keep you updated!" I blew a kiss towards the camera as Jacob waved goodbye.

Three hours later and I was in the same place as before, only this time surrounded by thousands of screaming girls clambering for the musicians' attention.

I'd watched the show countless times by now, however tonight felt different. Every time Theo and I made eye contact my stomach flipped. I felt just as giddy as the girls waving 'Mrs Theo Hart' signs in the crowd. But I loved the pride I felt, knowing that although so many of them wanted him, he only had eyes for me.

"Another great show tonight guys." I declared to the group, raising my bottle of beer in the air as we stood to side of the bar. "TVE tour part one - complete!"

"I'm surprised you're not sick of hearing the songs!" Callum laughed, clinking his glass to mine.

"Surprisingly not, I'm a fan first, blogger second!" I smiled, "where's Sean? I thought tonight of all nights he'd be with us!"

"God knows, he's been MIA a lot recently." Finn chimed in. "He's probably soaking up the attention." He rolled his eyes. Sean had always been self-assured for as long as I had known him but there had definitely been a shift in his ego in the last few cities. He revelled in the limelight to the point where he was now distancing himself from the band.

"Here he is, finally dragged yourself away from the cameras, have ya?" Theo shook his head, as Sean sauntered into the room, joining the circle we had made.

"It's not my fault the media loves me." Sean shrugged, clicking his fingers at the bartender for a drink, I shuddered slightly at his arrogance. "They only seem to care about your love life, T." My ears pricked up at his snide remark.

"What are you talking about?" Theo asked, slightly on the defence.

"Don't be stupid, you and Mils here, splashed all over social media." I felt the blood drain from my face at the new information. To my side Theo pulled out his phone and began searching his name in Google. Several articles popped up immediately questioning Theo's secret relationship with the band's blogger.

Shit.

"That was before we were even together for fuck's sake!" I ran a hand through my hair, staring at the images of us in Rome, before things had gotten heated.

"Before? So, there is a relationship then." Finn stated.

Shit.

I looked at Theo momentarily who resembled a deer in headlights. I took a deep breath before admitting it. "Yes, well no, well there's something here." *Wow, way to make a mess of that, Amelia.*

Theo chuckled, unaffected beside me before wrapping a calm arm around my shoulder. To my surprise the contact was comforting rather than petrifying and instinctively I melted into his touch.

"Sorry, this is how you had to find out, lads." A proud smile spread across his lips and it made my chest warm that he was happy to be seen as mine.

Finn nudged me on the shoulder. "Ahh nice one…To be honest, I'm surprised it didn't happen sooner."

"Hmm, so that's what I heard on the bus the other night then." Callum said quietly, as if recalling a previous event. I felt my cheeks heat at the memory of Theo pounding me on the black leather sofa. Note to self, no more sex on the tour bus!

"Anyway, one of the journalists outside was saying I'm the next big-" Sean began.

"Game of pool, anyone?" Finn asked the group cutting Sean's big-headed boast short. It would appear the topic of our situationship was now old news. I was quite relieved, I had been worried I would be treated differently if our connection came to light, so for the boys to revert to normal straight after the declaration, was a welcome surprise.

"Sure, I'll meet you guys over there, just getting us another round." Theo offered, taking my hand and squeezing it. No longer feeling the need to hide.

I walked with Callum, Finn and Sean to an unoccupied pool table and watched as the two of them began to rack up the balls.

"Amelia?" A familiar voice made my body tense up. I turned around and saw Josh standing behind me.

SHIT!

"Josh, what the-"

"Find my friends." He held up his phone which was flashing with my location. "I haven't been able to stop thinking about you."

"Don't-" anger boiled in my veins as his usual spiel escaped his lips.

"Please let me finish." I paused, allowing him to continue. "I fucked up. Big time, Aims, I was insecure and stupid about you travelling. I trust you. Please come back to me, I love you."

"You don't know what love is." I stated, bluntly. "For six years, you hurt me, betrayed my trust and treated me like your emotional punching bag. I never deserved any of that and I finally know my worth." I straightened up to him, standing up for myself for the first time.

"I'm confused Aims, it was a tiny fight, we've had worse ones and you've still forgiven me?" He argued pathetically. It was ironic, for all those years, all I wanted was for Josh to want me. To go above and beyond, surprise me, *prove* to me that I was his priority above all else but looking at him, forlorn in a pub in Berlin, I couldn't want him any less.

"That's the problem, Josh. This was never just about the travelling; it was always about you and your selfish attitude. We were stuck in a cycle of shit and I'm breaking it once and for all." My hands were shaking violently but I kept them clamped at my side. It was liberating to get this off my chest. "Why can't you just accept that this time it's over for us?"

31

THEO

It felt like a weight had been lifted. Even though this was not the way that I wanted my friends to find out about Amelia and me, or the world for that matter, I was overjoyed at finally being able to shout out that she was *mine*.

Just as I near on skipped around the corner to deliver the round of beers, I was stopped in my tracks at the sight of Josh and Amelia arguing. *Where the fuck did he come from?*

"All okay here?" I said, my jaw tensed as I announced my arrival to the scene. I was proud to see Amelia standing up for herself but wanted to let her know she had support if it was needed. The other three men were frozen, jaw wide, trying to blend into the background. I'm sure if needed, any one of them would have jumped to her defence but this wasn't their fight.

Josh's features hardened at the sound of my voice. Amelia stepped towards me and instinctively I reached to touch her shoulder. At the contact, Josh's rage ignited.

"What the fuck are you doing with my girlfriend?" He growled through gritted teeth.

"I'm not your girlfriend." Amelia spat from beside me.

"So, this is the real reason it's over then," he laughed maniacally, "christ, I knew you wanted her but the bed's still fucking warm mate and I never thought you'd lower your standards so much, Aims."

"It's been over for ages; just let it go." I kept my voice steady even though everything told me to rip this guy's head off.

"It's crystal clear now. You're a scumbag," he nodded at me, before pointing to Amelia, "and she's a slut." I saw red.

Before I could stop myself, I reached for Josh's collar and slammed my fist into his face. A satisfying crunch sounded as my knuckles made contact with his nose and blood poured from his nostrils.

"You need to learn when to shut the fuck up, Joshua." I pulled my hand back before punching him once again, this time causing a bruise to bloom on one of his cheekbones. "Keep *my* girlfriend's name out of your fucking mouth."

Josh choked out some kind of response, though I couldn't hear him over the sound of blood rushing through my ears. I felt four strong hands restrain me and

I let go of Josh's shirt causing him to stumble to the floor, grabbing at his broken nose.

I heard Finn and Callum trying to talk me down, still ushering me away from the crime scene. I shook their grip off and turned towards the exit only to be met with the wide eyes of Amelia. Her hands covered her mouth and she looked frozen in fear.

The red haze dissipated as quickly as it had appeared. "Sunflower…" I whispered, almost pleading for her to speak to me. I took a tentative step towards her, like I was approaching an animal I didn't want to scare off.

"Theo, I…" She shook her head. "Let's just go." I nodded, somewhat pleased she wasn't icing me out completely after the battering I had given Josh and the possessive title that had slipped from my mouth in the whirlwind of emotion. Although, anxiety still twisted in my gut as I tried to gauge her reaction to the violence.

"Can one of you make sure he gets to a hospital please?" She directed the question to my bandmates before joining me to head to a taxi.

We rode the car journey back in silence as I flexed my knuckles which were soaked in a mix of mine and Josh's blood. *What a stupid dickhead!* Amelia and I were finally in a good place and I had to go and fucking ruin it, smashing her ex's face in.

32

AMELIA

I watched the blood swirl down the sink as I wrung out the flannel I was using to clean Theo's knuckles. He hissed as I applied more pressure to the lacerations, the only sound he had made since arriving back at the hotel. We hadn't spoken a single word to each other since we left the scene of the crime.

It all happened so fast, I'd never seen Theo so angry. I wanted to stop the fight but I was frozen in place unable to comprehend what was happening. One minute I was talking to my ex-boyfriend, the next, he was a bloody heap on the floor.

I turned off the faucet and handed Theo a towel to dry his hands. The silence fell around us leaving unspoken words hanging in the air.

He looked up sheepishly from under his brow, his eyes heavy with emotion.

"I'm so sorry, Amelia." His voice shook, "I don't know what-"

"It's fine." I assured, releasing a breath I didn't realise I was holding.

"He was a prick but I shouldn't have done that." He rubbed the back of his neck, guiltily.

"You're right, he *is* a prick, and I'm glad you did that. Someone needed to knock some sense into him."

Theo looked shocked at my words, and I took in his appearance properly for the first time. Sitting on the side of the bath, shirtless and covered in the scars of defending my honour. I'd never wanted him more.

"That's fair but it wasn't my place."

"Well, if it wasn't going to be me who did it," I dried my hands against my clothes and stepped between his legs. He instinctively wrapped his hands around the side of my thighs. I stroked my fingers through his hair and gripped the nape of his neck before whispering, "I'm glad it was my boyfriend."

Theo's eyes filled with instant relief quickly followed by burning desire as he stood and claimed my lips in a passionate kiss that stole my breath away. Need swirled in my abdomen as the image of Theo standing up for me played on repeat. In one quick motion he had stood and lifted me up, I wrapped my legs around his waist, never breaking the kiss as he walked from the ensuite to the bedroom.

I felt the plush duvet beneath me as he laid me down. Wetness pooled between my legs as he slipped my trousers and underwear off.

"Take your top off, Sunflower." Theo rasped. I did as I was told and slowly pulled the fabric over my body. Theo groaned at the sight of me alone, his eyes drinking me in. Where I would usually feel insecure by being watched so deeply, I felt nothing short of beautiful from the way he was looking at me.

He crawled over me and my breath caught in my throat as I tangled my fingers in his dark brown hair, pulling his face to mine. I couldn't stop the moan from escaping from my mouth as he swiped his tongue along my bottom lip and began to make his way down my body. Sucking one of my hard nipples and pinching the other with his right, he positioned himself between my open legs.

"Say it again." He whispered, his breath ghosting over my needy pussy.

I quirked my head slightly, intoxicated by the proximity of his mouth to my core, my legs trembled with the need for friction.

He traced an impossibly light finger just above my clit. "You know exactly what I'm talking about."

My mind raced with snippets of our conversation, landing on the moment his expression changed. A smirk pulled at my lips before I purred, "my boyfriend."

A satisfied hum left Theo's chest before he leant down and licked a stripe between my slick folds. I threw my head back in pleasure. It's amazing how two words could make me feel so good. It had taken us so long to get here but I'd never been so sure of anything.

"Fuck, Theo, you're incredible." I almost sobbed as he lapped hungrily at my clit. He held my thighs open, his large hands gripping them tightly in a delicious mixture of pain and pleasure.

"That's my girl." He moaned against me, my hands, once again winding into his curls. I fisted his hair which only fuelled him further. He removed his grip from my legs and I began to wrap them around his head. "Nuh-uh, Amelia, keep them up for me."

I shivered at his demand and reopened them fully. I began to feel Theo's fingers entering me before curling up to find my most sensitive spot. He continued to work me towards my orgasm using both his hand and tongue. The mix of thick fingers and rough stubble at my core was sensational.

"I'm gonna co-" My stomach muscles tensed as the ecstasy coursed through my veins. Theo removed his hand, wiping his mouth with the back of it, before smiling at me devilishly.

I sat up on my elbows and stared him down. "Sit down, Theo, and take off your trousers." He seemed initially surprised at my dominance before unbuttoning his jeans and sinking into an armchair opposite the bed.

Slinking off the duvet to my knees, I began to crawl to him, Theo's eyes bulged at the vulgar image of me and I revelled in the way his gaze darkened.

"You are a fucking goddess." He panted, his hand making long lazy strokes along his cock. My mouth watered as I watched a pearl of pre-cum bead at the tip.

I situated myself between his legs and licked my lips. I had never cared much for foreplay in the past but what I had discovered from being with Theo was that I fucking *loved* sucking his cock.

I reached forward, trailing a finger along his erection, he moved his own hand away, placing them both behind his head.

"God, Sunflower, let me feel your wet mouth around my dick."

"Patience," I winked, wrapping my hand around his thick length. I leant my chest against his member before spitting between my breasts onto the head of his dick. Theo watched in awe, as I pushed them together, caging him in. "Who said anything about my mouth?"

"Jesus Christ, Amelia." I began to bounce my tits either side of him. He groaned, his head falling back on his hands on the headrest, though his eyes stayed glued to my breasts. This was so unlike me, I had never been particularly adventurous, but Theo brought out a filthy side to me that I didn't know existed until now. With each movement, he dissolved against the leather seat, moaning incoherently.

"Amelia, I need to be inside you. Now." His eyes darkened, there was no denying him what he wanted. He stood and began to walk to his bag beside the bed.

"What are you doing?" I questioned, the ache between my thighs, almost too much to bear.

"Condom." He said simply, rifling through the contents.

"I've got the coil. I wanna feel you." I spoke desperately. Although this wasn't our first time having sex, it felt different after our confirmed relationship status.

I sat down in the chair and draped my legs over the arm rests. "Fuck me here."

Theo's jaw dropped open as he let go of the handle of his bag and basically ran to me.

He cupped my face and placed a soft kiss to my lips. "Pinch me, I must be dreaming."

A giggle escaped me that quickly evolved to a moan as he lined himself up with my core and slammed into me.

The angle, the depth and the touch of his bare skin was otherworldly. I gripped tightly to his biceps as he pumped relentlessly - never breaking eye contact.

"Your cunt feels so good, Sunflower. Like it was made for me." His words pushed me over the edge, my climax taking me by surprise as it tingled from the tips of my fingers to the tips of my toes. My pussy clamped around him and I dug my nails into his arms, very nearly drawing blood. Theo upped his pace, chasing his own orgasm. An unexpected subsequent wave crashed over as I felt Theo release inside and I came around his cock for a second time as my mind blanked.

He leant his head in the crook of my neck for a moment before removing himself and scooping my limp body into his arms, carrying me to the bed. He laid beside me, pulling me into his chest, placing his free arm behind his head as we caught our breaths.

"Fucking hell." He scoffed with disbelief, shaking his head as if the past thirty minutes had been a blur.

"That was fucking insane." I stuttered out as my heart rate slowly returned to normal.

"You can say that again, Sunflower. I never knew you were so filthy." He laughed.

"Me neither to be honest." I giggled bashfully. "I never used to be."

A smug smirk pulled at his lips. "Only for me, hey?" I didn't bother to respond, still coming down from my orgasm, he knew the answer anyway.

We lay there, basking in the euphoria for an undetermined amount as he drew circles on my back with his fingertips.

"I can't believe the first leg of the tour is over." I said, gazing up at Theo.

"It flew by. So many amazing memories though and the ultimate souvenir." Theo kissed my forehead and butterflies erupted in my stomach. "Although a fridge magnet might have come with less baggage."

I slapped his chest. "Shut up, you love being my knight in shining armour." I laughed, sinking into his embrace.

"So, how's this going to work back in England then? I'm willing to take your lead but do I need to buy a black cap and hoodie to sneak in and out of your flat?" He was joking but I could tell there was a part of him that hated the idea of us being a secret back home.

And I hated it too which was why telling my friends had become more appealing, "I'm happy to tell the group but no announcements on your social media just yet. I still want to take it slow." If it hadn't been for the endless cycle of shit I had dealt with for the past six years, nothing would have stopped me from telling the world, but I couldn't deal with the looks and unspoken opinions again from people, if anything was to go wrong in the future.

"That works for me." He beamed, flashing a toothy grin. "As long as I get ample alone time with you, I'll agree to that deal."

33

AMELIA/THEO

AMELIA

I could hardly believe it but after months of planning and build up, Lilah and Zane's wedding had finally arrived.

Thankfully, the celebration had been scheduled to coincide with the break of The Velvet Echoes' tour, so Theo and I were free to attend without worrying about having to travel anywhere straight after or being late from a show.

We had been home for a few days and the group was still reeling with excitement from mine and Theo's news that we were in a relationship. Lilah was ecstatic that she actually liked the girl he chose to be with and Verity almost cried from 'how cute our story was'. Jacob, as ever, was jealous that I got to 'smash' Theo but was feeling rather pleased with himself as he had been gunning for an Amelia/Theo union from the get-go! However, that was old news in comparison to the wedding event of the year, minutes away from starting!

Jake, Verity and I waited anxiously in a grand room of the manor house that the wedding was taking place in. Verity and I wore identical emerald, green satin dresses and Jake's suit matched the colour perfectly. I twiddled my bouquet of peonies between my hands as we waited to see Lilah.

"There's the blushing bride!" Jake squealed as Lilah pushed the door open. The three of us were rendered speechless as she entered the room, ready to walk down the aisle.

I'd never seen a more beautiful bride. She looked like she had stepped straight out of an Italian bridal magazine. Layers of structured satin clung to her flame, bejewelled with intricate beading that accentuated her curves. The bottom of the dress flared out around the knee, in a fishtail style. The veil on top of her head trailed for metres behind her, covering her soft auburn curls.

"Oh, Lilah," Verity sobbed, desperately dabbing a tissue at her eyes to stop her makeup from running down her face.   I looked towards her before realising, I too, had streams of tears soaking my cheeks.

"You all look beautiful!" Lilah exclaimed, her own eyes welling up.

"Oh, don't you start!" Verity laughed, reaching for her best friend's hand.

"Not a patch on you. You're a vision!" I complimented. "Crap, my mascara, Verity, pass me a tissue please!" I snorted, noticing the black on my fingers from wiping away the teardrop.

"Yeah Lils, Jesus, I'm worried you're turning me straight! Can Zane fight?" Jacob interjected, causing the four of us to burst into laughter.

"Thank you all for being by my side." We all held hands, smiling like weirdos around the circle. Our love fest was broken by a light rap on the door. "Come in!"

The wood creaked, as Theo appeared. I was so used to seeing him in casual clothes that seeing him in a tuxedo, groomed to perfection, momentarily knocked the breath from my lungs.

"Stop drooling!" Jake stage whispered from beside me, nudging me in the ribs with his elbow.

Theo's eyes fixed on me as he walked over and placed a kiss on my lips. "You look incredible, Sunflower." I cringed for a moment knowing we had an audience but the warmth swelling in my heart, displaced any embarrassment.

"You too but hey, it's not about us. What about your sister?"

"Oh yeah," he turned on his heels to see his sibling, hands on her hips in mock frustration. "Meh you look alright, Lilah." He joked, giving her a hug and placing a kiss on her forehead. "Shall we go and get you married then?"

"Let's do this!" Lilah smiled, taking her brother's hand.

We all squealed before making our way to the ceremony room. We waited behind a large, closed entryway, listening to a string quartet play, my nerves rattling.

The doors swung open to reveal a large white room, covered in eucalyptus and white peonies. Rows of onlookers smiled towards us as we began to walk one by one down the aisle to the sound of the orchestra.

I drew the short straw and was placed first. I kept my eyes fixed straight ahead, trying to ignore just how many people were watching me, doing everything in my power to avoid tripping over and making a fool of myself. My heart almost burst as I approached Zane, who flashed me a nervous smile as he awaited his bride's entrance.

Verity, Jake and I took our places along the front row and watched as Theo and Lilah rounded the corner.

THEO

Lilah clutched my hand tightly as we watched her bridesmaids and Jake walk out to the waiting crowd.

"Careful sis, I need that hand to play my guitar!" I joked, trying to calm her obvious nerves.

"Sorry," she laughed, releasing her vice grip a little. "I don't know why I'm freaking out! I know everyone out there." She took a deep breath.

I turned towards her, taking both of her hands in mine. "Lilah, you have nothing to worry about. That man out there is completely besotted with you! It's just you and him in the room, don't think about anyone else." I said quickly, the time that we had remaining before our cue was diminishing by the second. The music reached a crescendo which signalled our turn.

"You ready?"

"Ready." She replied, flashing me her widest grin as she linked my right arm.

I was certain I heard every person in the room gasp as Lilah came into view. There was a possibility it could have been for me, but surely not on Lilah's big day, that would have been absurd!

Rows upon rows of smiling faces, watched in admiration as we made our way towards the dashing groom. I tried to take in the moment, but I couldn't divert my attention away from *her*.

Amelia looked otherworldly and I was so happy that I could call her mine to everyone here today. It would have killed me to watch her from afar, pretending we were just friends, allowing any single men in Zane's genetically perfect family to kid themselves, that they stood a chance with her.

She was glowing, the light radiated around her hair like a halo, which was styled perfectly into an updo with loose tendrils cascading around her face. Amelia caught my eye and I flashed her a quick wink, causing a coy smirk to spread across her face before breaking the contact.

After what felt like forever, we reached the altar. I let go of Lilah, placing a kiss on her cheek before reaching out to shake Zane's hand. "Best of luck, *amigo*."

"Thank you, *hermano*." Zane responded, before turning his attention to his bride. I moved out of the aisle and took my place to Zane's side as the registrar began the ceremony.

We took our seats as she red the rehearsed speech, giving a brief history of their relationship and asking if anyone here knows of any lawful reason as to why these two should not be married today. Giggles filled the audience as Lilah performed an overexaggerated phew action when no one stepped forward to derail the wedding.

After the ceremony drew to a close and Mr and Mrs Moreno were officially announced, everyone cheered for the happy couple. A few hours later, after canapes and cocktails and my *amazing* best man speech, we were all settled, ready for the wedding breakfast. Various Colombian dishes were spread across the circular tables, paired with the most delicious wine from Zane's native country.

With our bellies full and heads beginning to swim from the alcohol, it was time for the groom's speech.

Zane stood up from his chair at the sweetheart table, releasing Lilah's hand that he had been holding and reached into his pocket to retrieve a folded piece of paper.

"*Buenas noches* everyone! Firstly, I would like to thank everybody for being here today. This day wouldn't be anywhere near as special without our friends and family present." He gestured around the room as the guests clapped. "And thank you to our bridal party for all your help throughout the planning process." Another round of applause began in the dining hall. I turned to my side, to smile at Amelia who was already grinning

back at me. "But most importantly, my dearest Delilah."
Here we go, time for the most romantic speech in history!

"Where to even begin? We met when I was only seven years old and my life was inexplicably changed. Albeit we barely spoke, except for the pranks I carried out at your expense, yet I never stopped thinking about you. When our paths crossed years later, it was almost as if fate had intervened, bringing you back into my life. We've grown together, laughed together and worked together - although you were a subpar PA and I was an unprofessional boss."

Cheers and laughter erupted from the guests as Lilah blushed with embarrassment. I was aware that their relationship had begun in the workplace, but I didn't need to think about what those two had gotten up to in the office. Which was confirmed all the more by Jake winking at Lilah as if he knew all the dirty details!

Zane turned to my sister, taking her hand in his, ignoring the fact there was a room of one hundred people behind him. He only had eyes for her. "You complete me. You are my better half. My business partner, my life partner - my forever. I don't know what I did to deserve you but I thank my lucky stars that we are here today and you'll always be by my side. Standing beside you as your husband is the greatest honour of my life." Zane's voice cracked and a surprising lump formed in my throat. I reached over and squeezed Amelia's thigh. She turned to me, tears filling her eyes also.

"Please raise your glasses to my beautiful bride. *Tu eres mi Joya, mi vida, mi amor* and now my wife. I'll love you for all time, Delilah Moreno." Zane turned his attention back to the emotional crowd, lifting his wine flute into the air, "*¡Salud!*"

"*¡Salud!*" We all repeated in unison. The sound of clinking glasses and animated chatter chorused around us.

The remainder of the evening flew by in a blur of good music, good food and copious amounts of Colombian rum. From the moment the music started, I never left the dancefloor. Twirling and dipping Amelia all night long surrounded by our closest friends.

With my sister and my best friend looking the happiest I'd ever seen them and my perfect girlfriend as my date, it really was a night that I'd never forget.

34

THEO

It had been a month since Amelia and I had become official and still the words 'my boyfriend' falling from her perfect lips were like magic to me. Since being back in England, we spent our days avoiding the paparazzi and evenings wrapped up in each other.

Despite Amelia's hesitation to announce our relationship to the prying eyes of the media, after the wedding I'd had the honour of meeting her family - a milestone I had never reached with another woman before.

I shifted my weight from one foot to the other, trying to play it cool as we waited outside Amelia's family home to be let in. I noticed Amelia shooting me a sly look out of the corner of my eye.

"Spill it, Sani." I chuckled, turning to face her. "What's on your mind?"

"Oh nothing. I'm just enjoying seeing Theo Hart nervous for once." She giggled, reaching for my hand and rubbing soothing circles on the back of it. Her touch alone calmed my anxieties.

"I only get nervous for things I really care about." It was true. I'd never cared about anything more. Forget the arenas and screaming fans, the only two people in the world that I cared about impressing right now were her parents.

"Don't worry, they don't bite." She nudged me slightly, *"they're gonna love you, Theo."* She implored when I didn't have a usual cocky retort.

I smiled at her, reaching to stroke a curl behind her ear and pulling her face towards me in a delicate kiss. Her lips moved against mine and I felt myself getting lost in the sensation.

"Ah, you must be, Theo!" A friendly voice broke whatever spell Amelia had me under and I jumped away from her abruptly. How I didn't hear the door open I will never know.

Amelia laughed at my side, *"hey Dad."*

I'd never met two more welcoming people, the whole afternoon was like spending time with old friends as they reminisced on stories of Amelia's childhood and we told the story of how we'd met, before exchanging memories from the different countries we had all visited. I returned from my daydream and began scribbling down the lyrics in my notepad, before running through the song once again. I sang the words that I had just written down:

> *You're a wildflower,*
> *Blooming where the fire once burned.*
> *You're a golden hour,*
> *The light within you's returned.*

You're a sun-

The movement through the glass window of the studio cut my session short. I stopped strumming my guitar and looked up to see Amelia's angelic smile beaming at me from the sound desk.

"Hey rockstar." She purred, through the intercom. "What are you writing? Sounds like it's about someone special." She teased.

"Hello, gorgeous." I smiled, clenching the pick between my teeth. "Can't you see I'm recording?" I gestured towards the illuminated red light.

"Carry on, then." She rolled her eyes, giggling.

"It's not done yet, Sunflower." I explained, feeling somewhat embarrassed at the thought of performing an unfinished song to her.

"I want to hear it." She insisted, sitting on a stool and crossing her legs. I could see through the glass that her skirt had rode up slightly and I swallowed through the dryness of my mouth as I looked at her bare thighs.

"Anything for you, I guess." I chuckled before resuming my rehearsal, the melody filling the room.

"So yeah, as I said it's rough." I concluded as the song came to a close.

I hadn't looked in Amelia's direction once as I played but now the song was over, I stole a glance, only to see her stock still with admiration.

"Theo…you should sing more often!" She gushed. I felt my chest puff with pride and my heart swell at her complimentary words.

"Ahh, no. Sean is the vocalist of the group." I waved her off, moving the guitar to the side of me. "I wouldn't want to step on his toes." I rubbed a hand across the back of my neck, feeling exposed. As much as I loved attention usually and I knew my lyrics were good, singing them solo always made me feel incredibly vulnerable.

Amelia opened the door of the recording booth and I instinctively reached for her. She swaggered towards me and I tried not to drool as I watched her hips sway before she situated herself between my legs. I caressed the sides of her thighs and she melted under my touch, smiling so sweetly at me I could have sworn I'd get a toothache.

"So, you never answered me…who's that about?"

I smirked, tugging on the bottom of her denim skirt causing her to stumble against me. "Don't play dumb, Sunflower."

"Go on, I like it when you tell me." She pushed my hair back, leaning closer to me. Her sweet scent was intoxicating and I couldn't wait a minute longer to be with her.

"Yeah, well I like it when you take my cock like a good girl." I growled in her ear, before wrapping my arms around her waist and lifting her onto my lap. I heard her release a breath before pressing my lips to hers in a passionate kiss.

Amelia succumbed to my touch, our tongues fighting for dominance as her fingers wound their way into my hair. Her skirt rode up and she ground against me, each gyration causing my cock to harden further.

"Fuck, Mils." I moaned which only spurred her on. "I fucking need you."

"Take me then." She breathed and I nearly came in my pants. The effect this woman had on me was like nothing I had ever experienced before. Why people took drugs, I would never know, as the high I got from Amelia was better than any narcotic.

Without further instruction I stood from my seat, lifting Amelia with me. She wrapped her legs around my waist and I brought us towards the soundproof wall of the recording studio, never breaking our kiss.

I reached between us, moving her panties to the side, shivering at the feel of her underwear, drenched with arousal.

"You're so fucking wet for me, Sunflower."

She mewled at my words. "Please, Theo."

I unbuckled my belt with one hand, still keeping Amelia pressed against the wall, unsheathing my dick with ease.

I slid into her, her pussy felt like velvet surrounding my length. We groaned in unison and I buried my face in the crook of her neck.

"Goddamn, Amelia." I growled before sucking a sensitive spot above her collar bone.

"Don't leave a mark." She instructed breathlessly, although the protest sounded weak.

"I want everyone to know you're mine." I concluded, kissing the bruised skin, branding her for all to see.

I continued to pound her relentlessly whilst finding her clit with my right hand. I rubbed circles across her sensitive bud, eliciting needy moans from her which only fuelled me on further.

"That's it baby, I want you to come all over my cock for me." Without a second's hesitation I felt her cunt constrict around me. Each pulse of her centre was like a shock wave through my body as I held my own orgasm back. Thrusting desperately to keep her at the peak of her climax.

Once she had come down from her high, I swung her around, pushed the door of the small room open and carried her through, placing her on the sound desk.

She squirmed against the hard buttons. "I can't fucking believe you're mine." She panted, her brown eyes blinking up at me with so much love I almost couldn't handle it.

"The feeling is mutual, sweetheart." I slammed into her, harder than ever before and fucked her relentlessly until she was a whimpering, boneless heap on the mixing table. This woman, who I had been so infatuated with for so long, was finally *mine*. And here she was dissolving under my touch. I released into her, watching every reaction on her face as she came in time with me. I wanted to remember this. I *needed* the image of Amelia climaxing against me burned into my retinas.

Our heart rates slowed and vision returned, wrapped up in each other's arms, sweat sticking to our clothes from our frantic escapade.

"You should visit the studio more often."

35

AMELIA

I stood with the band outside the offices of their music label. I'd never seen a building so tall in person before. It was a glass pillar shooting out of the ground towards the sky.

"Let's go guys. I don't think he's coming!" Callum called towards us as the band and I walked into the foyer, deciding not to wait any longer for Sean to make an appearance. We were given passes before riding up the elevator to meet with the band's manager, Gary.

"Alright lads, how's it going? And, Amelia, lovely to meet you in person finally." We shook hands and I took a seat on the leather sofa, in between Theo and Finn. Instinctively, Theo took my hand in his and entangled his fingers with my own. I froze initially at the contact, although the boys knew, I wasn't sure whether Gary or the rest of Theo's management were aware of our secret. "No Sean?" He questioned but didn't seem surprised by his absence.

"Nope, he's ghosted again. Something's off with him, man." Theo shrugged, running his free hand through his messy hair. Since being back in the UK, Theo had mentioned Sean was flaking on their band meetings more and more, which seemed odd for Sean given how much he loved being the centre of attention and hated missing out on anything.

"Well, I'm busy so I won't waste time waiting for him to take his career seriously." Gary responded, matter of factly. "As you are all well aware, the second leg of the tour kicks off in a week, this time we have ten dates around the UK and Ireland, so prepare for a little less sunshine than you got on the continent!" He chuckled at his own joke, "to be honest fellas, I have very little notes for ya. The fans are loving you; streaming stats are through the roof and you're on track for your album to hit number one in the UK charts next week." The band cheered and high-fived each other. I was so proud of them all, they really had worked their arses off to bring their music from the ground to the top! "And, Amelia, your diary. It's been so successful; the clicks and advertising sales we're getting are beyond our wildest dreams. Thank you for your hard work."

I couldn't stop the stupid grin from spreading across my face at his compliments. I was so pleased that the time and effort I had poured into the blog was paying off for everyone.

For the next hour, Gary ran through the itinerary of the tour, interviews and photoshoots the boys had scheduled along the way and the wrap party that he had planned when the show culminated in Dublin.

"Thanks for your time, can't wait for a Guinness when this ends in a month or so." Gary concluded as we all began to stand and file out of the room.   "Theo. Amelia. Can you stay for a moment please?"

"Sure, all good mate?" Theo asked, with confusion in his eyes, as the rest of the boys filtered out, closing the door behind them.

"It's no secret that you two are together and I'm happy for ya, honestly. But maybe when you go back down to the adoring crowd, keep it under the radar. Get it? Under The Radar?" He laughed again at his subpar joke. The use of my blog name as the punchline to avoid people finding out about Theo and I's relationship made my stomach churn. I had been the one that wanted to keep this under wraps for as long as possible but for someone else to encourage that, as if I could damage his career, was heartbreaking.

"Thanks for the advice." Theo said simply, before we turned to leave. We stepped into the lift in silence, as I let go of Theo's hand. "Are you ok, Mils?" He asked. I could see the concern across his face from the corner of my eye but I couldn't bear to look at him, in fear that I'd burst into tears.

We left the hotel, to be met with swathes of screaming girls all ranging in age. They chanted the boys' names, sang Theo's lyrics and snapped selfies with the members as the guys did their best to give each person as much attention and care as possible.

"Theo! I love you!" I heard a girl who couldn't be much younger than me, calling towards *my* boyfriend. She ripped her shirt open to expose her chest, "sign here." She trilled, lust coating her words. Theo laughed awkwardly before shooting a glance in my direction. I shrugged, as if I had a choice in the matter. At the lack of decision from me, Theo faced the woman again, uncapped the Sharpie with his teeth and signed his name across her breasts.

Watching him interacting with his fans, knowing he could drop me in a second for any one of them and tear me to pieces was terrifying. I hadn't felt this type of jealousy before. In Europe, they met fans all the time - the majority of which were women who were begging Theo to marry him or trying to steal a kiss as he moved along the queue of people, waiting for even just a millisecond of his time.

But it felt different then. Maybe it was because I hadn't admitted to myself what I was beginning to understand now. I was falling for him. Harder than I ever could have imagined possible. And the power that he held over my already fragile heart petrified me.

36

THEO/AMELIA

THEO

I caught myself humming an unwritten tune as I basted the steaks in a pan, the smell of garlic and rosemary flooding my small kitchen. Amelia rounded the corner, wearing one of my old band T-shirts as a nightie and a towel wrapped around her hair.

"Wow, that smells amazing, Theo. What's the occasion?" She padded towards me, wrapping her arms around my torso from behind.

"Just treating my girl." I smirked, turning my head to kiss her on the cheek. "I appreciate the hug, Mils, but I can't stand an overdone steak." She laughed and released her grip, allowing me to remove the meat to rest. "Nice shower?"

"Mmhmm, would've been nicer with you in it." She purred.

"You're relentless, Amelia." I spanked her on the arse and she squealed slightly.

"You bring it out of me." She winked before walking over to a cupboard across the room, retrieving two wine glasses. "It's still so odd being here without Lilah." She mused, placing the glasses on the table.

"Bet you never thought you'd take me up on the offer from the first time you were here, did ya?" I chuckled, bringing the two plates over. She looked at me, puzzled. "Second door on the right." I smirked, reciting the words I had spoken to her one of the first times she was here as a guest of Lilah's. She rolled her eyes; in the same way she had all those years ago. But this time I leant forward and stole a kiss.

"And you say *I'm* relentless!" She breathed, leaning away from me, we took our seats and began to dig into the gourmet dinner I'd prepared.

"This is incredible! Exactly how I like my steak." She beamed at me.

"I do try." I took a sip of wine, anxiety suddenly swirling in my gut at what I had prepared myself to say all day. "Amelia." I started, her chewing slowed and her dark eyes met mine.

"Yeah."

"I didn't know the best time to give you this." I reached into my pocket, retrieving the freshly cut key. Amelia's vision latched onto it and she put her cutlery down. "I know you want to take things slow, so it's not a moving-in key, it's just an I'm-serious-about-this-and-you're-always-welcome key." I placed the key between us on the table and awkwardly rubbed the back of my neck waiting for her to say something. Anything.

"I don't know what to say," Amelia began, picking up the metal and twirling it between her fingers as if assessing it was real. "This is so kind but surely you wouldn't want me swanning in unannounced." She avoided eye contact with me, looking sheepish. In that moment, it had dawned on me that in six years with Josh they had never made it this far, so why would I appear legitimate to her after such a short amount of time?

"That's exactly what I want." I took her hand in mine, "look at me." She flicked her gaze up to meet mine. "This isn't a fling for me, Sunflower. I've never felt like this for anyone. Damn, I get giddy just hearing your name. For years I watched from the sidelines, wishing I could prove to you how you should be treated. I still can't believe that you are mine and there's no way I'm letting you go." Her eyes were so round, so surprised, for the first time in our relationship I couldn't read her thoughts.

"Well, if you're sure then I accept your key. Watch out for the surprise 3am break ins." She laughed, slightly awkwardly, like she was trying to keep the conversation light.

"Can't wait," I rubbed a circle on the back of her hand with my thumb. "Seriously, Amelia. I'm crazy about you and I just have to say it out loud." I took a deep breath before the words spilled out of me.

"I love you."

AMELIA

The words hung in the air, "you don't have to say it back." He reassured, breaking the silence and I realised I had been staring blankly for a beat too long.

"I really want to, Theo, but I-" My voice shook with unwelcome nerves.

"I get it, it's okay. There's no rush, Sunflower." He squeezed the hand he was holding. I wished I could give him what he deserved. Theo had always been so open with his feelings, but I wasn't ready to be quite so transparent, given my history.

I hated the way my brain had been conditioned to deflect any form of love. Even now, he couldn't have responded any better to my reaction. I was so used to having to walk on eggshells and hide my true feelings around He-Who-Shouldn't-Be-Named, but I knew I didn't need to with Theo, so why couldn't I tell the truth now?

God, Theo really is too good for me.

"Hey, you still with me?" Theo's voice sounded distant and I shook my head to rid my clouded thoughts.

"Yeah, sorry. Just took me by surprise."

"That's me, Mils, I'm full of 'em." He winked and I instantly felt myself relax, glad that I hadn't ruined the evening with my inability to function in a relationship.

I love you. I love you. The words rung in my head desperate to get out but one day at a time.

37

THEO

"Theo, no way!"

A semi-familiar American accent called out. A hand found my bicep and I turned to see the brunette woman I'd met in Amsterdam.

"Amy!" I said with realisation, wrapping my arms around her in a friendly hug. "What are the chances?"

"I guess we can't stay away from each other." She flirted as I released her. *Uh oh, gotta douse this fire.*

"Ha, what brings you to London?" I swiftly diverted the conversation.

"I've got friends here. This is gonna sound stalker-ish but I'm actually going to your gig tomorrow." She giggled, her cheeks flushing red slightly.

"Oh really? Paying for your ticket this time?" I joked, causing her blush to deepen.

"No, I actually thought if I hung around the streets of London long enough, I'd bump into you and we could pick up where we left off." She took a step closer, running her hand down my chest and hooking a finger into the gap between the buttons and the shirt.

I recoiled from her touch and brought my hand to hers, moving it away.

"I'm afraid that's off the cards, Amy." I smiled, not wanting to be too harsh with the girl. It's not her fault I used her as a distraction in Amsterdam.

She looked a little awkward for a moment before replacing her pout with a small knowing smirk, "ah, so the rumours are true." She said, with no malice. "You and Amelia are good together."

I couldn't hide the grin and the pride I felt being associated with her. "I know." I agreed simply before checking my watch. "It was great to bump into you again, Amy, but I've got to dash I'm afraid. Enjoy the show tomorrow!"

She gave me a quick peck on the cheek. "I'll wave to you from the rafters, rockstar."

I turned on my heels and carried on down the road towards Finn's.

"Sorry I'm a bit late guys, you'll never guess who I bumped into when I was walking here." I apologised to Callum and Finn as I entered the flat.

"The King." Callum said in jest.

"Elvis is long dead mate." Finn responded deadpan.

I raised my eyebrows at Callum, "joking mate, who?"

"Amy, the girl from Dam." I took my jacket off and slung it over the back of a chair.

"Oh yeah, I remember the girls in Amsterdam," Callum's words trailed off as if he had gotten lost in the memory of his raucous night with two girls and his best mate.

"Small world!" Finn interjected.

"Incredibly small. She's actually coming to the show tomorrow in Edinburgh."

"Ooo how's Amelia going to feel about that?" Callum needled, passing me a beer.

"What?" I queried, "why would she care? I didn't invite her and she won't be coming backstage. Chances are they won't even cross paths and I made it clear to Amy, this ship has sailed."

"Aww poor girl, bet she left in tears." Callum joked.

"Fuck off." shaking my head with a grin, I settled into the beanbag on the floor. "No Sean again? At this rate I'd be surprised if he even made it onto the stage tomorrow night."

It was the night before the UK and Ireland leg of our tour was due to kick off and we were meeting up to finalise details of the setlist and cheers to another few weeks on the road.

"Ah come on, yeah he's flaky but he always comes through in the end." Callum stuck up for his buddy.

As if he was summoned, Sean sauntered through the door.

"See, told ya." Callum nudged me with his foot, reaching out to hand Sean a beer.

"Nah, I'm good, Cal." He shook his hand in protest. "I'll keep this nice and quick, lads." He clapped obnoxiously, remaining on his feet, towering over the three of us.

"What are you on about, Sean?" I asked, narrowing my eyes. I had a feeling I wasn't going to like where this was going.

"It's no secret that I'm the talent, the most popular and not to mention the eye candy of this band." I had to force myself not to scoff at the arrogant perception of himself. "I've been having talks for a few months now, with another record label. They wanna sign me solo and let's face it, it's about time I dropped this dead weight." Sean flung his hand out towards us as if reciting the words that had been blown up his arse to convince him to cut loose! Callum, Finn and I's mouths fell open at the declaration.

"Without this 'dead weight', you wouldn't even have the offer you prick." I bit back, shocked by the audacity of him to insult the three people that got him to where he is now. "How are we meant to get through the next few weeks knowing you're fucking off at the end?"

"Oh, you'll be fine, I'm not coming. Take this as my formal resignation." He laughed at his own stupid joke. Like now was the time to be a fucking comedian. "I start recording my debut album next week in LA." He said smugly, like any of us gave a shit.

There was silence for a minute but the sentiment from myself and the rest of the boys was ringing loud and clear.

Is he fucking joking?

"Ah, well we'll miss ya mate." Callum stuttered, as if he hadn't fully registered the weight of Sean's confession.

"Miss him?!" I exploded, standing up and turning towards Callum. "He's leaving us high and dry the night before we go back on the road and you'll fucking *miss* him!"

"He's clearly made his mind up," Callum stood too, gesturing towards the prima donna.

"Yeah, but we don't have to be happy about it!" Finn joined us on his feet. "It's a fucking piss take."

"Easy fellas, maybe you can be my support act when I go on tour."

"Dream on, I've read some of the lyrics you write." I scoffed knowing damn well his discography would be worlds away from ours. There was a reason I was the songwriter; his lyrics were about as deep as a puddle.

"No need to get emotional, Theo, you're just jealous they asked *me* and not you." He smirked and I balled my fists at my side.

"I've never had any interest in being a frontman or a solo artist. You guys are my family, I would never fuck you off for money or fame." I felt a lump form in my throat. As much as Sean and I had our differences over the years, these boys had been some of the closest people in my life. Knowing that was all about to change was devastating.

"Yeah man, we all knew you could be a prick but we never thought you'd betray us." Finn spat.

"Don't let this ruin your tour guys, it'll probably be your last one now I'm out of the picture." Sean sniggered.

"You should leave before I fucking knock you out, mate." I shouted, the rage inside me bubbling up.

"Easy, easy. I'm going." He saluted us before disappearing through the door. The three of us stood like statues, static ringing in our ears as we processed the fact that our lead singer had quit the night before a show.

"So, what now?" Finn asked, his eyes wide as saucers, staring at me as if I had all the answers.

"I need to think." I ran a hand through my hair, bemused at what had just occurred. Sean had come in like a six-foot wrecking ball and left us all shell-shocked. "I need to go, I'll see you both in the morning. Sorry."

38

AMELIA

My heart stopped as I flicked through a series of photos of Theo and a certain, beautiful brunette that had been published on the popular celebrity gossip site, StarBuzzDaily.

Immediately, I recognised her to be the woman Theo had gotten to know on tour, the night we had argued and I had broken up with Josh.

He had assured me on the tour bus that nothing had happened between the pair of them but seeing that she was on the same street in London as my boyfriend, I found that hard to believe.

A lump formed in my throat as I stared at the pictures of Theo and Amy hugging, Theo and Amy holding hands, Theo and Amy…clearly about to kiss.

I had been waiting like the dutiful girlfriend in Theo's flat, for him to come home, from the band meeting he had told me he was going to, only to be jump-scared by paparazzi photos on my feed.

My stomach cramped with anxiety as to the possibilities of what the cameras hadn't captured. Why was she here? Had Theo invited her? Why would he lie to me?

I rang his phone. No answer. Each ring made me more nauseous. Tears began to fall down my cheeks. I thought Theo could be trusted but now I realised I had been fooled once again. I'd trusted someone before who had betrayed me countless times and used my forgiveness to hurt me further. And despite knowing the signs, somehow, I had let myself get blindsided again. Bile swirled in my stomach as my breaths became shallow and my vision blurred.

My body took over and I hurried towards the hallway to retrieve my belongings. I slipped my shoes on and began to reach for my coat before a key in the lock made me jump.

"What a fucking shit show." Theo said, releasing a deep breath as he shrugged off his jacket and moved towards me. "I'm so glad you're here though. Come here baby." He entangled me in his arms and I felt myself go rigid. His proximity making me feel uncomfortable for the first time. "What's up?" He pulled away, his hands remaining on the tops of my shoulders. He glanced up and down my body, "why are your shoes on? And you're holding your coat? Wait, you're crying?!" His voice was flooded with anxiety.

"Just tell me the truth, Theo." I whispered, barely able to verbalise my demand.

"Is this about Sean? I'm confused." He laughed awkwardly, trying to ease the tension. The sound caused my anger to spike.

"The photos, Theo." He released his grip from my arms, his expression becoming unreadable.

"Please enlighten me, Sunflower." He asked genuinely which only twisted the knife further.

"There were photos of you on your little date." I threw my hand in the air and sniffled, trying, and failing, to regulate my emotions.

He stood for a moment, mulling over my words as if replaying the past few hours in his head. "Ohhh, you mean Amy?" He asked, realisation painting his features.

"Of course I mean Amy. Unless there are others you need to tell me about too." I snapped, rage taking over.

"Whoa, whoa, whoa…take a step back. What do you think is going on here?" He was the picture of innocence. No wonder he'd managed to pull the wool over my eyes for so long.

"I'm not going to spell it out for you, you fucking idiot." I exploded, firing on all cylinders. My words knocked the air out of him. I unlocked my phone with shaky fingers, turning it to show him the evidence. "It's clear from these."

Theo took the device, the silence deafening as he was faced with his infidelity.

"Oh, Mils, don't be silly. I just bumped into her."
I felt my cheeks heat with fury as he tried to downplay
his actions.

"Then explain the photos, Theo. This looks more
than a casual chat." I gritted my teeth, trying not to let
more tears fall.

"They want headlines and clickbait but I assure
you, Amelia, there was nothing untoward in that
interaction." He handed my phone back before reaching
out to wipe a stray tear off my cheek. I flinched away and
he mirrored my action, looking pained that I hadn't
allowed him to touch me.

"Yeah, they want views but they didn't force you
to hold hands." I waved the phone in his face.

"That's a stretch, Mils; I'm clearly moving her
hand away. We were talking about *you*!" He pleaded,
willing me to believe him.

"What about?" I shouted in disbelief. "How
much you're going to enjoy fucking her again behind my
back?"

"Again?!"

"Amsterdam, Theo."

"I never slept with her in Amsterdam, we literally
just kissed and then I called it a night." My heart
dropped.

"You're a fucking prick." I choked out between
sobs. "You told me nothing happened." I was vibrating.

"I told you I didn't *sleep* with her." He raised his
voice to match mine. "But even if I had, Amelia. We
weren't together."

I shook my head. "But we are now, and that clearly didn't stop you tonight. You never went to Finn's, did you?"

"What the fuck are you talking about?" His voice broke. "I have *never* given you a reason not to trust me, why are you holding something against me that I've *never* done? I would *never* hurt you, Amelia, you have to know that?" His anger had gone, replaced only by sadness as he stretched a hand out to touch the top of my arm.

"I believed that once, Theo. Yet here we are." I shook him off, passing him to get to the exit and shrugging my coat on.

"What can I do to prove it to you?" His plea was a punch to my gut.

"That's the thing, Theo, you can't." My chest constricted, my breaths becoming more shallow.

"Don't tar me with the same brush as Josh. I'm not him." He protested. I saw red and swung the door open. How fucking dare he use my ex-boyfriend as a scapegoat for his actions.

"I have to applaud you, Theo." I turned back from the doorway to face him, "for so long you made me feel like you'd have done anything to be with me. I guess the thrill of the chase was more intoxicating than actually having me. Well congratulations, now you'll never have me again." I scoffed, delivering the killing blow and slamming the door behind. The force of which shattered my heart into a million pieces.

39

THEO

As the sound of my apartment door clapped shut, my legs gave out and I crumbled to the floor.

I pulled my knees into my aching chest and sobbed, the image of Amelia leaving etched into my eyelids. I wasn't sure how long I laid there, motionless, but it was dark outside by the time I dragged myself upright again.

My body moved of its own accord, towards the door to follow Amelia to her place and beg for her back but I knew before I approached her again I needed to process what the fuck had just happened.

Resigning myself to misery, I uncorked a bottle of rum that Zane had gifted me after the wedding and took a hearty swig, straight from the spout. The burn in my throat barely even touched the searing pain coursing through every inch of my body.

Fuck. What am I gonna do?!

For the past few years, it'd always been Amelia. Whether I was at a party, searching for her face, to flirt up a storm with until she batted me away or more recently, tracing the contours of her body after making her my own, I didn't know life without her anymore.

I had always promised to protect her, to shield her from any hurt. Now here I was, alone, after I had inadvertently broken her heart. The idea of her being in pain was worse than my own. Especially considering she was adamant I had committed the ultimate betrayal.

I ran a hand through my hair and caught the time on my watch.

3.32am.

I had to be up in less than four hours. I trudged through the flat, haunted by the ghost of Amelia. From the lip-stained glass on the bedside table to the crumpled-up band t-shirt she had borrowed from me last week, her presence was everywhere, even if she'd only been a handful of times.

Slipping into the cold sheets, her scent clung to the fabric, knocking me sideways. I needed to sleep. I wanted to wake up in the morning and this all have been a bad dream. As I rewound the events of the evening, a lump reformed in my throat and I dissolved into sleep with tear-soaked cheeks and a painful chest.

****

"Cor, you're taking Sean's departure pretty hard aren't ya mate? I was closer to him." Callum laughed, lounging on the sofa on the bus opposite me.

We had been on the road for a few hours and besides initial greetings, I had kept myself to myself for the journey so far unable to strike up colloquial conversation with the guys, given my inner turmoil.

I watched as Finn nudged him in the ribs and overheard him whisper to Callum, "shut it mate, have you not noticed who else is missing?"

"Ah fuck." Callum muttered looking around us as if only just now noticing Amelia's absence, "I'm sorry mate, I didn't even realise. I was being selfish." He directed an apology to me.

"Not your fault." I shrugged. Stupidly a small part of me was optimistic that she would have been waiting at the pickup point this morning, ready to put this whole misunderstanding behind us. But as the sun rose and we piled our bags into the bus, there was no Amelia.

"What happened?" Finn moved to sit beside me and put his arm around my shoulder.

"She saw paparazzi photos of me and Amy, that didn't capture the best angles and she assumed the worst." Saying it aloud was like reliving the night and a sharp pain shot through my chest. I picked at the fabric of the sofa, avoiding eye contact with the guys.

"Dude, what the fuck?" Callum exclaimed. "I don't get it; she was with Josh for year-"

"Can we not?" I interrupted. "I don't really feel like talking about it."

"Sorry, T. Here if you want to chat but we know you'd never hurt her." Callum responded sympathetically, leaning across the gangway to tap my leg. I nodded in thanks, it meant more than I could say that the band was there for me. Well, the remaining members of the band at least.

"Appreciate it mate, let's hope she realises that soon too. Anyway, let's talk business." I clapped my hands together, trying to focus my thoughts on anything but my heartbreak. "We step on stage at 8pm tonight and currently we're performing fifteen instrumentals. Any ideas?"

Callum and Finn exchanged a look as if they'd already had this conversation without me. "To be honest mate, we just assumed you would do it." Finn announced sheepishly.

"Well, that's good to know but why?" I laughed slightly though it felt wrong to do so, like the vibrations through my chest were causing the shards of my heart to twist uncomfortably.

"You wrote all the songs, so no one knows them better than you!" I think Finn meant that as a compliment but I'd never felt so nervous.

"And we can't sing." Callum interjected, matter of factly.

"I mean, I do know all the notes and tracks for the lead but fuck, I'd never thought about being the front man. I much prefer brooding, background singer." I chuckled awkwardly, "but I guess I've got no choice?"

"Not unless you want all the tickets to be refunded when I start barking down the mic," Callum joked, starting to sing '*Accidentally*' awfully off key.

"But obviously if you're not feeling up to it, we can work something out." Finn reassured.

"Nah, it's cool. I'll put my big boy boots on." Perhaps the nerves would overshadow the anguish.

"Obviously this would only be short term, presumably we'll need to get on the lookout for a new singer pretty sharpish." Callum advised, picking at the edge of his nails.

"Yeah, I'll reach out to Gary and ask him to get some auditions set up or something." I responded, as weird as it would be to replace Sean, maybe some new blood would be good for us.

Hours later and I was backstage in Edinburgh, anxiously anticipating my lead singer debut. The two guys huddled around me as we prepared to take the stage.

"No matter what happens, we've got your back. You're not alone out there." Callum called over the roar of the crowd as the intro music came to a close.

"Love you boys." I declared to my two best friends. "Let's fucking do it!" We put our hands into the middle of our makeshift circle and raised them into the air before running out to the screaming fans.

A statement had been issued just before the show to announce Sean's departure but I'd been too nervous to read any of the responses on social media. However, looking out at the sold-out crowd, I was relieved to see

the arena was still full and supporting the three of us
without him.

A strange silence filled the room after the screen
lifted to reveal the new trio. I played the opening riff of
our first song and opened my mouth to sing, praying that
the lyrics came out in some comprehensive manner.
Glancing at Finn who had now made his way to the
drum set, I caught him throwing me a wink as he began
to set the rhythm. One deep breath later, I closed my
eyes and sang.

The surge of noise that followed was almost
deafening and cleared any worries that I'd had only two
seconds prior. As the crowd went wild, I relaxed into the
music and hurtled my way to the end of the opener.

"Good evening, Edinburgh! How are we
tonight?" I called out to the fans, my voice coming out
surprisingly calm. "I know we probably don't look exactly
the way you hoped for tonight, or sound for that matter."
A flurry of giggles rippled through the auditorium, "but
we thank you for still coming out and supporting us. We
love you guys and don't wanna let you down but please
expect some hiccups and surprises as we navigate this set
list." A second wave of 'awws' followed. "You ready to
have some fun? We're The Velvet Echoes and we're so
happy to be here in Edinburgh, let's go!"

We stumbled through the remainder of the setlist;
I fluffed my lines at times and fucked up chords but the
crowd and the band never abandoned me. Considering
the whirlwind of emotions that I'd been through, I didn't
think I'd done too badly.

As we took our final bows after the encore, I instinctively glanced to the edge of the stage, where a certain brunette had occupied in Europe and the vacant spot broke me, bringing me back down to Earth with a bang. It was ironic that after all the adrenaline this evening, the first and only person I wanted to debrief the night with was the one person who had left me alone and heartbroken.

40

AMELIA

For the past three days I'd been disconnected from technology, I didn't have it in me to see photos from the gig two days ago or to face talking to any of my friends about Theo's deceit. It was embarrassing that I couldn't find a man who wanted me enough to not need a side chick.

I thought I'd experienced heartbreak before, but this was million times worse than anything I'd dealt with in the past. Every part of my body hurt, even breathing felt like a laborious task.

A sharp ring at my doorbell made me jump. I wasn't expecting or *wanting* company.

I peeled myself off the sofa and tentatively opened the door only to see the faces of my three best friends.

"Hello darling," Jacob greeted, "let's go and have a chat, shall we?" He moved towards me, wrapping an arm around my shoulder and guiding me inside as Lilah and Verity followed carrying wine and flowers from what I had spotted quickly in the doorway.

The four of us settled onto the sofa and floor cushions in my living room. I took in the sympathetic and confused faces of my friends. I had been adamant until now that the last thing I wanted was the emotional pow wow that seemed to occur every time one of us was heartbroken but having them here proved me wrong.

"What did he do?" Lilah interrogated, no doubt assuming Theo was in the wrong. "I'll fucking kill him." I wanted to laugh at her joke. Instead, a sob crawled its way up my throat and erupted into the room.

"Oh babe." Verity cooed, pulling me into a hug, that for once I didn't resist. "Was it really that bad?" The knife twisted harder.

"I-I," I stumbled over my words, "I saw these pictures of him and another woman and I-"

"Pictures?" Jake asked. "Pictures of them doing what?" His voice was urgent.

"See for yourself they're on StarBuzzDaily. I'm surprised you've not already seen them, Jacob." I bit back, more aggressively than intended.

"Easy tiger, I'm not the enemy here. I'll get them up now." I played with a curl, instantly feeling bad for biting my best friend's head off.

"I'm sorry. I'm a mess right now." I sniffed as Jacob reviewed the evidence and passed it around the group.

"Were they a fan?" Verity asked, tentatively.

"No. I wouldn't care if they were a fan." I sighed. "They met and probably fucked in Amsterdam and it seems he invited her back for round two. Or God knows how many rounds they've done." I couldn't stop the anger bubbling through my veins as I verbalised what I had been trying to forget for the past seventy-two hours.

"What the fuck!" Verity exclaimed. Lilah assessed the picture, chewing on her lip slightly.

"Surely there's more to this?! He worships you." Jake looked confused.

"Fucking seems like it doesn't it." I scoffed, sarcastically. "All I know is that I can never trust him again." I didn't know it was possible to cry that much but I could barely form a sentence through my tears.

My friends sat in silence, unsure of how to console me. Over the varying years I had known them all, this was the most emotion I had probably ever shown.

"I'm so sorry, Amelia. Theo's been avoiding my texts, I assumed he was guilty of something but never expected this, what a prick." Lilah mulled over her thoughts.

"I saw fans online talking about how he's been acting differently which I just assumed was because Sean left and not because he's a cheating scumbag." Verity added. "Sorry, Lils!"

"Hey, no defence from me, he's an arsehole." Theo's sister added.

"What do you mean Sean left?" I questioned, surprised. Where I'd been living in the dark ages, I'd missed any showbiz news.

"Ah yeah, Sean quit the band the night before the first gig back. Bit of a mess really but Theo stepped in." Lilah interjected, filling the gaps in my knowledge.

Classic Theo saving the day and being the band's hero. Always painting himself in the image of a white knight!

"How did you all know anyway? About me and Theo?" I asked, bemused at how they got the information considering my radio silence.

"When we saw no tour diary entry last night our suspicions were raised and then when there still wasn't one today, it was even more glaringly obvious that you hadn't gone. Given that you're never late posting and you're the hardest working person we know!" Lilah advised, squeezing my knee.

"So, we knew we had to come and check everything was okay." Verity added.

"For a minute we thought you were dead, so I have to admit, heartbreak is the preferable discovery of the two." Jake chuckled, making a 'phew' action.

"Jake!" Verity and Lilah exclaimed in unison. I couldn't help the laugh that escaped at the absurdity of Jake's statement.

"I'm so sorry babe. Just know, you're not alone and we'll stay as long as you need us to. Men suck." Jake assured, pulling me in for a hug. "And I know you're hating every second of this hug, but I love you."

Verity and Lilah joined us in our embrace. "I love you all too."

41

THEO

I should feel ecstatic to be playing the largest gig in my hometown but without Amelia there, I felt hollow.

The silver lining was that Lilah and Zane would be in attendance, which was sure to be a nice distraction.

Lilah had asked to meet me prior to the show and as I opened my dressing door, I couldn't help the smile forming on my face at the sight of my little sister, swaying back and forth in the swivel chair.

At the creak of the door, she looked up, standing to greet me.

"Missed you, sis."

"You too." She said curtly.

I ruffled her hair, ignoring her unexpected standoffish attitude. "Where's the Colombian God then?"

"For fuck's sake, he'll be here in a minute, forgive me for wanting some sibling time before you're distracted by your boyfriend." She rolled her eyes and we moved to sit on the seats in my room. "Shall we address the elephant in the room?"

"Ah, I assumed this was what you wanted to meet to talk about." I sighed, bracing myself to bring up the painful subject.

"Why didn't you tell me?" She implored, lowering her voice.

"She's one of your best friends, Lils."

"Yeah exactly, why the fuck would you cheat on her?"

I took a deep breath, trying to dull the pain that had formed in my stomach, at the realisation, that Lilah thought I was capable of hurting Amelia in that way. "Lilah, please, you have to believe me. I didn't."

"I saw the photos, Theo. It doesn't look good."

"You're fucking telling me." I laughed but there was no humour behind it. "It was a complete fluke that I even bumped into her. I was telling Amy that I was with Amelia now and there was no chance of anything happening between us. You know how the paps are, Lilah."

Relief crossed my sister's features, followed by pity. "Theo, she's so convinced."

My heart shattered all over again, my shoulders dropping in defeat. "Please if there's any way of getting through to her-"

"You'll be the first to know." She implored. I gave her an appreciative half smile.

"Thank you for believing me." I pulled her off her seat into a much-needed hug, finding comfort as she wrapped her arms around me.

"You're my brother and you're the only family I have. I will always be there for you." I swallowed past the lump in my throat formed by her words. Lilah and I had become closer in the years we only had each other.

"I'm fucking lost without her, Lils."

There was a hard knock on the door, and I blinked back the sudden tears, breaking away from Lilah before Zane's face appeared round the frame, as he opened it.

"I'll leave you boys to it." Lilah placed a kiss on my cheek, "good luck out there. I'll be cheering you on!"

"Thanks, Lilah. For everything." I called to her as she passed Zane.

"Ah *mi amigo*, aren't you a sight for sore eyes!" I turned my attention to the six-foot stallion, wiping the tears away that had escaped down my cheeks.

Zane rolled his eyes at my awful Spanish, before bringing me in for a quick hug. "I heard everything at the door. You know I'm a man of few words but I'm sorry about Amelia and I'm proud of you for stepping up for the guys."

"Thanks bro, means a lot."

"Go and knock 'em dead superstar." Zane hyped me up. I paused for a moment, shocked at his frivolity. Zane was always so strait laced and buttoned up.

"Well one of us needs to bring the Theo energy."
He laughed, tapping me on the shoulder, before leaving
me alone with moments to spare till show time.

The gig started like any other: adoration from the
fans; adrenaline from the atmosphere; and
encouragement from the rest of the band.

It was a boost to see Lilah and Zane side of stage
as I sneaked looks to see if Amelia had arrived – given
this show was in London, a tiny part of me held on to the
hope that she might have come to reconcile.

I moved out towards the runway on the stage,
taking a seat on a single stool. The spotlight shifted and
my heart flew to my throat. In the shadows, I was certain
I could see the silhouette of Amelia.

Whilst singing the next song on our setlist, I
didn't divert my eyes. Hoping, praying, that the lights
would shift to confirm that she had come to end this
torture.

The crowd erupted into cheers and applause as I
finished the tune. I had become surprisingly comfortable
in my new role but was thankful for the day I handed the
microphone to our new recruit - who we were still on the
search for.

I began to introduce the next song, '*What If*'. The
song that meant so much and was intertwined in the
history of our relationship. The lights lifted to illuminate
the crowd so I could speak directly as I described the
emotion. As the pink and blue lights cast a glow over the
faces below me, pain struck me full force in my gut as I
realised what I had tried to deny. There was no Amelia. I

had conjured the figure in the darkness only for the light to drive home the truth.

She wasn't here. It was well and truly over.

42

AMELIA

In another life, I would have been across the city, watching Theo and the guys perform to a sold-out London crowd and celebrating the success of the night into the early hours.

Instead, Verity had come round to keep me company to prevent me from wallowing too deep into my self-pity and confiscated my phone, so I would avoid the streams of content from the local show.

The last thing I needed to see was Theo having the time of his life on stage with throngs of girls begging to bed him, whilst he decided which one or more he would be choosing to wile the night away with.

Eventually I drifted off, changing one grotty slouchy top for a fresher one.

After a couple more days of moping around, I decided I should think about reaching out to Lilah or Zane about going back to Moreno Hart Jewellery. I was certain my days of blogging for indie bands were well and truly over after an excruciating phone call with Gary, yesterday, since I left them high and dry.

Whilst typing an email to my bosses in an attempt to be professional, an unexpected visitor knocked on my door interrupting my request for paid work.

I stood from my seat at the table, where I had been typing on my laptop. As I approached the door, it clicked open of its own accord, startling me. Standing frozen in the middle of the room, I awaited the intruder to be revealed.

"Hey babe," Jake announced as he casually sauntered into my flat.

"What the fuck, Jacob, you nearly gave me a heart attack!" I clutched my chest.

"Oh, chill out, I've got a key to all of your places in case of emergencies and this," he gestured at my unkempt appearance, "is a code red emergency!"

I rolled my eyes, "thanks Jacob, I feel so much better."

"Glad to hear it, but we needed to talk asap. Sit!" He instructed, and I followed the instruction, sinking into the couch.

"I've been thinking," he started.

"Good for you, I've been trying not to…"

"There is no way on God's green Earth that Theo would cheat on you." He announced, matter of factly.

"How can you be so sure that he didn't?" I sighed, not wanting to have this conversation.

"Lilah called me after the London gig. Theo is in bits babe, he swore blind it wasn't what it looked like and told her everything. Why would he lie to her? In his mind, he's already lost you."

"Jake, I know what I saw." I insisted.

"No babe, you filled in the blanks of what you wanted to believe." He gave me a stern look, cutting me to my core.

"Why would I want to believe Theo cheated on me?" I argued back.

"Because it's easier than admitting that you love him." The realisation hit me like a ton of bricks. Was it possible that I had projected this story onto Theo in a roundabout way of protecting myself? I never knew Jake was such a good therapist but him spelling this out to me was slowly untangling the mess that was my mind. Tears pricked at my eyes.

"You were looking for a reason to break up with him as you were scared. I know how you've been treated before and it's understandable why you would want to protect yourself, but this is Theo we're talking about. He's a living angel." The honesty of his words stunned me. "I think you should give him another shot or at least a proper chance to explain himself. If you still don't believe him, then that's your prerogative."

Jacob's words consumed me, swirling around my mind as I processed what he was saying. How could I have been so blind? So stupid? To believe the static captures of some paparazzi images and not the declaration of the man, who had only ever proved himself to be loyal and caring, at every possible occasion?

I had tarred him with the same brush as Josh, as he had made me believe that the only love I was capable of receiving, was a love that came with a huge side dish of betrayal and anguish. How I ever could have thought him and Theo belonged in the same box was beyond me.

The sobs were coming more frequently as I thought over the way I had spoken to my ex-boyfriend. He never deserved any of the insults I hurled his way. *I* was the arsehole. "I just-"

"Don't deny yourself something worth fighting for, cause of the shit that last dirtbag put you through." He sat on the sofa beside me as my tears continued to fall. My mind darted as I thought of my next move.

"I would obviously never say this to you if it wasn't plain to see that you love the boy." His voice softened and he flicked at the t-shirt I had on, "you're wearing his sweaty top for fuck's sake." I hadn't realised but absentmindedly, I had put on one of the shirts he'd left behind. Although I'd never said the words to Theo, even when he'd declared it to me himself there was no denying, I was wholeheartedly in love with him and had been for longer than I'd realised.

"I can't, Jake, I just can't." The tears soaked my cheeks as I released all the pain I had been burying deep down.

"What's holding you back? Don't let your pride or your fear for that matter, stop you from finding the happiness you so deserve." He clutched my hand tightly as I shook. He was right, all Theo had ever done was love me and I threw it back in his face. I had never deserved him; I had judged him at the first sign of betrayal and broken both of our hearts.

"He misses you, Amelia. He would never ever hurt you. I can assure you of that and if he has a lobotomy and forgets how to treat you, I'll rip his balls off and you can feed them to any animal you wish."

I couldn't help but smile at his declaration. The scary truth of it was that I was certain that it was not an empty threat.

"I'll leave you be," he kissed me on top of my head and stood from the chair, "you've got a plane ticket to buy."

43

THEO

Since Sean's departure, Gary had been trawling through the masses of entries that we had received from thousands of budding male singers, who were all interested in replacing Sean as our frontman.

Callum and Finn had mainly been screening the hopefuls, both digitally and in-person where possible, who had been deemed worthy by our management. I trusted them to narrow it down to the best of the best. Besides, I had enough on my plate at the moment, the last thing our prospective new member needed was me moping behind the desk as they sang their heart out.

The boys had assured me that I needed to meet a guy called Ezra who conveniently heralded from Ireland. Which was our next - and last - stop of the tour.

We had arranged to see him the day before our final show for an in-person audition and to see if he gelled well with all three of us. I was nervous. Even though I wasn't the one auditioning, he had to like us just as much as we had to like him - what if he was great but thought we were all a bunch of idiots. God, it felt even worse than a first date!

The three of us sat behind a fold out table in the conference room of our hotel, looking like a budget version of a judging panel from a reality talent show.

"Oh my god, have you seen? Sean has announced his new single. Didn't take him long." Finn scoffed holding up his phone, that he had been scrolling through.

"Fucker." I said under my breath. He had clearly been planning his exit from the band for much longer than we had realised. "Can't wait to compete with him in the charts." I laughed sarcastically, not worried in the slightest.

"Watch this space," Callum winked.

The double doors opened and a man, who I presumed to be Ezra, walked in. He was effortlessly cool; I could feel the air shift from his presence alone.

He must have been over six foot, dressed simply in a dark pair of jeans and a half unbuttoned, patterned shirt which showed a glimpse of a tattoo underneath.

"Afternoon lads, I'm Ezra Reed, nice to meet you." He greeted, walking forwards to shake each of our hands.

"You too mate. We're excited to see what you've got for us." I replied.

"Well, I've actually got one of your songs to sing, hope you don't think I'm trying to kiss your arse too much." He laughed, "I really was a fan of you guys before the opportunity came up."

"Don't apologise, Theo loves praise." Callum ribbed on me and I shoved him playfully.

"Good to know," Ezra responded. Their natural banter was clear to see. "Can I borrow that?" He pointed at my acoustic guitar, leaning against the wall. I nodded in agreement.

"Take it away, fella." Finn encouraged. Ezra slung the strap over his shoulder, tested it was tuned and took a deep breath before starting to perform.

It was strange to hear my lyrics sang back to me from someone other than Sean but I had to hand it to the guy. Ezra captured the emotion and meaning behind every word, in a way in which Sean never seemed to before.

I couldn't help but tap the table along in time with the song, perplexed by his talent. Every note was perfect, his voice was angelic yet rough and his strong Irish accent slipped through on occasion adding to its uniqueness. A few minutes later he had finished. He replaced the instrument and moved back to the centre of the room to hear his fate.

"So that was that," he chuckled awkwardly, clasping his hands together in front of him.

The three of us looked at each other and telepathically communicated what we all agreed upon.

Personality: check
Looks: check
Talent: check.

"Ezra mate, that was great but you know we've seen a lot of people." He took a deep breath; it was clear to see how much he wanted this. "I'll be honest, I do have a concern," I saw the guys to my right, looking at me surprised as if I had misunderstood their eyebrow raises and smirks a moment ago, "I'm concerned that you're gonna end up with more fans than me!"

"For fuck's sake," Finn burst out laughing.

"I wish he was joking." Callum added. Ezra looked surprised. "What he's trying to say is, you're in the band!"

"Oh wow, thank you, this is so exciting!" Ezra ran a hand through his dark, curly hair seeming unsure of what to do with himself.

"Come here mate, you deserve it. That was a knockout." We met him in the middle and huddled for a group hug.

"So next steps, we're planning to launch the new line up at our headline gig at Glastonbury in June." This was going to be our biggest show to date, so there was no more perfect a time to announce Ezra's arrival. "Until then, we have our final show of our tour tonight in the city centre and we'd love you to be a guest backstage. Come along, meet the crew, get a sense of the adrenaline cos it won't be long until you're getting it first hand on the big stage!"

The four of us continued to chat through plans, hype each other up and get to know Ezra a bit better before we needed to head to the arena.

As we drove to the auditorium, I recalled the past few months of our first European tour. The highs were out of this world and I was beyond thankful for every opportunity but I couldn't deny that I'd never felt lower than I did now.

44

THEO

The three of us ran off stage to the sound of the outro music. The crowd was electric, the arena was almost shaking from the stamping and demands of an encore. Even so many shows down the line, the feeling was yet to sink in for us, that so many people loved our music and came night after night to see us perform and share in the magic with us.

"You're fucking smashing it pals," Ezra called over the deafening noise of the fans metres away.

"Thanks mate, I can already imagine the sound of the crowd when you're introduced!" Finn shared the compliment.

"Can't wait." He responded simply. "Now get back out there before those girls storm the stage." The crowd was deafening as they screamed for more.

Callum, Finn and I, wrapped our arms around each other, ready to share one final band huddle.

"You guys are two of my best friends in the whole world and I'm so thankful that I've been able to share this experience with you both. Ezra, get in here!" I broke the circle and invited him to join us, "things are only going to get better from here and I can't wait to do it with you both and now with our new buddy, Ezra. Let's take over the world boys!" We cheered and threw our arms up before a quick embrace and back to the waiting crowd.

"Okay, okay, calm down, we'll give you one more!" I said through the microphone to raucous applause. "Seeing as it's the last show of our tour, we thought you deserved a special treat." More screams exploded, threatening to burst my eardrums. "This is a new one that I'd written whilst on the road this year. It's a special song to me, about someone who has been my inspiration for years. Although they're not here to hear it firsthand, it only felt right that I played it for you all tonight. This is for you, Sunflower." My voice was thick with emotion as I held back tears.

The crowd turned silent and I began to play. The beginning of the song was acoustic and calm, just me and my guitar as I sang the lyrics I had performed for Amelia, in the studio, only weeks prior. My heart ached as I recalled the memories of the start of this year. Her laughter in Lisbon as we celebrated her birthday, her tears in Amsterdam as she pushed me away, her smile as we finally gave into each other in Berlin. The scenes flashed through my head like a cruel but beautiful montage.

As I reached the chorus, the tempo lifted and Callum and Finn joined in on their respective instruments. The crowd erupted with the melody and began dancing along, enthusiastically. Considering they didn't know the song; they reacted like it was their all-time favourite.

The song perfectly captured how I had fallen for Amelia. From the slow painful yearning to the vibrant, all-encompassing free fall of loving her. The only difference was this song had a happy ending.

I moved into the second verse, beginning to look more confidently at the crowd, knowing the song had been well received. My eyes moved along the edge of the stage as it had done so many times before and fixed onto a sign that took me by surprise.

ONLY HERE FOR THE FIT GUITARIST

My heart stuttered as I read back the words that I had once joked with Amelia about, telling myself that it must be a coincidence, yet standing below the large white card, was my girl.

I was certain she was another mirage, a cruel trick that my brain was playing on me. But as she continued to smile widely, shaking the sign, I knew she was real. As our eyes locked, it took everything in me not to stop performing immediately. In the darkness of the auditorium, she was like seeing daylight. I was transfixed as she turned the sign around to show four simple words in black pen.

I LOVE YOU THEO

At that moment, I stopped singing and placed the guitar on the floor.

Jumping off the stage, I ran to her waiting for the image of her gorgeous face to disappear and prove I really was insane.

To the soundtrack of Callum and Finn, continuing the score of the song I had abandoned, I took Amelia's face into my hands and stared at her dumbfounded.

"Are you real?" I gasped, taking in every detail of the face I had longed to see once again.

"Everyone's watching," she giggled, glancing around at the thousands of eyes now trained on us, accompanied by just as many phones snapping this unique moment.

"I don't fucking care."

Unable to wait a second longer I crashed my lips against hers, it was like breathing after drowning, like pleasure after pain. I wrapped my hands around her waist, feeling the contours of her perfect body. "I fucking love you, Amelia." I breathed between kisses.

"I love you too, Theo."

45

AMELIA

"Go back and finish the song, I'll be waiting right here."
I laughed, the first genuine laugh since I had walked out
of Theo's flat.

"Not a chance, Sunflower. I can't wait another
minute." He smirked, kissing every visible part of skin on
my face and neck as camera phone flashes illuminated
around us.

Theo turned to the crowd, from our spot
between the barricade and the stage, raised his arm up in
a silent goodbye and turned back to Callum and Finn as
we made our way along to the exit. We cleared the length
and Callum flashed a wink at Theo as he continued to
play the song to completion.

We exited to a chorus of cheers and applause
before we were finally alone backstage.

"Wait," I said, stopping Theo in his tracks. "I just
need to get this off my chest."

"Go ahead, Sunflower. I'm all ears." Theo encouraged, holding my hands in the darkness of the backstage area.

"I believe you, Theo." Relief spread across his face at my declaration, "I do and I'm so sorry for judging you against the actions of someone else." He squeezed my hand. "These past four months have been life changing. Without you, I would never have gotten the opportunity to live out my dream job. Without you, I would never have realised the type of love I deserved and without you, I couldn't live another moment. I've never felt this way in my life and truth be told, it petrified me Theo. I've been used and abused before but never have I been wholeheartedly loved. You gave me that in spades and rather than embrace it, I ran away. Well, I don't want to run anymore. I understand if you don't want to give this another shot, I spoke to you terribly." Emotion clogged my throat.

"I'm not going anywhere." Theo couldn't contain his smile as a single tear rolled down his cheek, I wiped it gingerly.

"I love you, Theo Hart, for longer than I care to admit, perhaps even when I shouldn't have but I'm ready to jump in with both feet and ride this journey with you."

My declaration was interrupted by the band running off stage and the crew celebrating the completion of the tour.

"Let's go back to your dressing room, we can chat privately there." I suggested although I was already being pulled there from an eager Theo.

We walked into his room and I was thankful to find it empty.

"Theo-"

"Shhhh," he claimed my lips and pushed my body against the wooden door, slamming it shut, "I'm done talking."

His hands roamed my body desperately as if feeling my curves for the first time. I hooked my fingers around the hem of his t-shirt and pulled it over his head to expose his hardened abs. I'd forgotten just how ripped he was, moisture pooled between my legs.

God, I'd fucking missed him.

"I've fucking missed you." He gasped verbalising the words in my head, before dropping to his knees. His hands slid up my legs, pushing my skirt up as he went.

"Theo, I need to make it up to you, not the other way around." I said weakly, his breath ghosting over my underwear, making me shiver.

A devilish grin formed on his face, "I haven't tasted your sweet cunt in way too long and I'm starving." Jesus if words alone could make me come, I'd already be a limbless pile on the floor.

I submitted as he slung one of my thighs over his shoulder. His strong fingers pulled my lacy underwear to the side and his tongue expertly found my clit.

My head connected with the hard wood behind me as I let out a guttural moan. Theo continued to work me to oblivion, never coming up for air.

I dug my nails into the tops of his arms as I came with full force. "Sit down." I ordered breathlessly as Theo hastily moved to the leather sofa.

I fumbled with the buttons of his trousers, pulling them and his boxers down to reveal his full length, hard and ready for me.

I stepped away from him, he groaned frustratedly, longing for my touch.

I giggled before slowly removing my dress. His eyes watched me hungrily as the fabric moved inch by inch up my body.

"Fuck, Amelia, am I that predictable?" He moaned, taking in the black lace bodice I had worn especially for the occasion. "You knew I'd take you back, huh?" He smirked as I stalked back towards my prey.

"Guess so." I winked, failing to think of anything particularly witty to say while he was looking at me like that.

Lowering myself to my knees, I wrapped a hand around his dick and began stroking along him before taking him into my mouth completely. I gagged as the head of his cock touched the back of my throat causing Theo to groan needily.

"Your mouth feels like heaven." He breathed no louder than a whisper as I continued to bob my head up and down. Glancing up occasionally, I met Theo's eyes, wild and desperate. Just seeing the look on his face was enough to send me towards my second orgasm. I slipped my free hand between my legs, finding the sensitive bud and moved my fingers in time with my movements on

Theo, as his hand tangled between my curls, my second orgasm built to an agonising peak before dissipating through every nerve ending.

"Now that's not fair is it, Sunflower?" he purred. "You've come twice and I thought you were the one who was supposed to be apologising." He winked cheekily. "Come here."

He pulled me onto his lap as he laid down on the couch and once again, manoeuvred the lace out of the way. He slid his rock-hard cock into my begging core and pushed into me, deep and long. I paused for a moment, adjusting to his size before the need to ride him overwhelmed me.

"I *am* sorry, Theo." I whispered, seductively, leaning close to his ear.

"How sorry?" He gasped between the thrusts.

"Incredibly." I rocked my hips back and forth, my clit making contact with his groin.

"Oh yeah?" He goaded, I began to bounce up and down. His hands found my breasts, squeezing and pinching my hard nipples.

"Theo. I'm going to come again." I almost sobbed, willing Theo to follow suit.

"Go ahead, angel." He encouraged, causing the tingles in my stomach to intensify.

"I need you to come with me." I begged, my movements becoming jerky, my body feeling more his than mine in that precise moment. "Please, Theo. Come inside me."

My words must have triggered something within him as he let out a loud moan of my name mixed with curse words as I felt him release. My core tightened around his cock at the same time and I near on screamed at the blinding pleasure.

"I love you, Amelia." Theo sighed, pressing a kiss to my sweaty shoulder, as we both came down from our highs. I hummed in contentment.

"I love you, Theo."

"Mmm, I could get used to hearing that."

After a blissful moment, I reluctantly rolled off him onto the sofa. He pulled me close to his side, not letting me be more than a few inches from him.

"I hope this room is soundproof." I was suddenly all too aware of the ruckus we had been making for the past half an hour and how many people would be roaming the corridors of the arena now that the show had finished.

"It's not even a little bit." Theo laughed. The sound of his chuckle was like a warm hug, enveloping me and soothing the heartbreak that I had foolishly bestowed on myself for the past few weeks.

As I lay beside the love of my life, who was tracing patterns along my bare back, I was unable to feel embarrassed at the prospect of being heard.

He was mine and I was his, just as it was always meant to be. Given half the chance I would have shouted it from the rooftops as I was no longer consumed with the fear of breaking down my walls and giving into this feeling. All I cared about was Theo and the life we had ahead of us.

EPILOGUE

AMELIA

"Five minutes to stage lads." One of the stage managers called to the band as we all waited nervously backstage at Glastonbury Festival. Not only was this the largest summer festival in the UK but it was set to become The Velvet Echoes largest (and no doubt loudest) crowd to date!

I watched as Callum, Finn, Theo and their new singer, Ezra formed a huddle, hyping each other up before they were due to face the horde on the other side of the screen, who were waiting to catch a glimpse of the front man who had yet to be revealed to the world.

Nervous energy bubbled inside my own gut as I watched the newly formed group give each other a pep talk. I hadn't attended any of their rehearsals as I had wanted to experience this moment just like any other fan of the band, so the feeling was exhilarating as I waited to see their energy on stage.

Admittedly, it was odd to see The Velvet Echoes without Sean but seeing Ezra laughing and joking with Theo and the two guys I had gotten to know so well on tour, they honestly looked like a perfect match.

Pride and love swelled inside of me as I watched Theo's dreams on the cusp of skyrocketing to new heights.

Over the past month, my dreams had also begun to come to fruition. Thanks to Theo's support and the growing popularity of my blog, I was on the way to opening my own record label. Only last week did I acquire the keys to my new office building.

"You need to get a sign made and put it right here." Theo *gestured to a blank space above the doorway when he came with me to pick up the keys and move in some immediate furniture. "Under The Radar Records, I can see it now." He moved his arm in the air as if imagining the words forming in front of his eyes.*

"I agree, it's the perfect spot. But that's not the name," he looked at me confused, "and I've already got a sign." I slid a large brown box across the floor and ripped open the side to reveal a bright yellow emblem.

"Sunflower Records." Theo read aloud slowly, registering the words as he said them before looking up at me shocked.

I shrugged, smiling shyly at him, "I couldn't have done it without you." Theo whisked me into his arms.

"It's perfect, Sunflower."

My chest warmed at the memory. I was so excited to get everything set up and get to work finding and helping out all of the undiscovered artists that traditional, larger labels might overlook.

Theo and I caught each other's eye across the room. "One minute to go." The same manager from before shouted. The other boys all took their places, holding instruments and microphones nervously. However, Theo didn't join them. Instead, he bolted towards me and scooped me into his arms, claiming my lips in a chaste kiss.

"Good luck out there my fit guitarist." I giggled, blinking up at him with stars in my eyes.

"I'll be looking for ya." He winked, before kissing me again and joining the rest of his bandmates.

The signal was given and the group ran animatedly onto the stage, to roars from the crowd.

My stomach was in knots for the next hour and a half, as I watched as the band commanded the stage. Theo divulged in his signature moves, flirting with the crowd and making jokes which caused all the girls to swoon however it was clear to see, with every glance back in my direction, that he only had eyes for me.

As I watched his career reach new heights in real time, I reflected back on our less than conventional journey. How we started as friends, with undeniable chemistry, to dates disguised as birthday outings and stolen moments behind closed doors, our love had been far from straight forward. It was complicated, emotional and confusing but never on Theo's side. I didn't know what I had done to deserve him. I was far from perfect, but I was imperfectly perfect for him.

ABOUT THE AUTHORS

Ria Alice and Jessica May are two friends from the UK with a shared love of steamy romance novels. Their books contain pop culture references galore, fun, supportive friendships and spicy relationships to top it all off!

When they're not writing, you can find them at a 2000's emo night, a karaoke bar or marathoning cheesy rom-coms over a charcuterie board.

Keep up to date with their latest projects on social media:
Instagram: @authorriaaliceandjessicamay
TikTok: @riaaliceandjessicamay

BY THE AUTHORS

THE HIDDEN SERIES
A series of interconnected standalones

Hidden Gem
Hidden Agenda

ACKNOWLEDGEMENTS

Wow! Here we are, book three of the Hidden universe.

When we were planning the series out, almost a year ago, Talent was the one that we could picture from the get-go. We knew Theo and Amelia were endgame even when Lilah and Zane were our primary focus.

We pictured Theo's declaration in the bar; Amelia's defiant break up with arsehole Josh; and knew Theo would be counting those climaxes even back then!

Seeing their story come to life has been amazing and we've loved digging deeper into our cool girl, Amelia and golden retriever, Theo. We wrote this book over huge chapters of our own lives, (Ria's son turned three and Jessica got married!), so it'll always be one that's close to our hearts and reminds us of great memories.

With the final book on the horizon, we're excited to get to know, two relatively unknown characters and learn even more about our favourite fictional band, The Velvet Echoes.

Now to the thanks! As always, thank you to our partners for going to bed solo, giving us up for weekends or generally having to hear how much we "love Theo" for months on end. We wouldn't have finished another one without you both.

Thanks again to our beta readers who provide invaluable feedback, time and time again and ultimately help to make the story the best it can be!

Lastly, thanks to you for reading our THIRD novel. We hope you loved the nods to one and two and are enjoying seeing our gang progress as the series goes on.

Now let's crack on with the finale, shall we!